REED

Kate Allenton

Discover other titles by Kate Allenton

At

www.kateallenton.com

ISBN-10:
1-944237-13-5
ISBN-13:
978-1-944237-13-4

ACKNOWLEDGMENTS

I'd like to acknowledge my
READERS....You all rock.
Thank you for taking a chance on my
books.

1 CHAPTER

Reed Love popped a handful of Skittles into his mouth as he scanned the pictures on the Internet, trying his best to block out the extra boxes of private information that popped out at him.

With his ability, what he could see was similar to the pop-up ads that companies paid a pretty penny for, but the data in these boxes were things any normal person would be mortified he had access to.

He was more than a computer genius and hacker extraordinaire, thanks to his DNA. He had a love-hate relationship with the invisible boxes and the ease of access. It was as if his mind was melded with all of the information on the internet and coded with the algorithms. The electronic information that people thought was safe would appear in boxes around their person, even if he was just looking at a picture. Pictures, financial data, passwords, it didn't matter what the information or how deep in the web they tried to disguise it. Reed had access, no matter if online or in public. These boxes danced in front of him, enticing him to look.

His mind worked like a direct link to the Internet hub where all data was stored. All he needed was the right trigger to reach inside and be able to pull out the file. Unlike Mike, he wasn't a human lie detector. But like his sister, Skylar, who could see streams of energy for everything, Reed saw the code, and his mind processed it with images.

He didn't enjoy knowing everyone's secrets. He didn't thrive on the damage that could be done. The only thing in the world he wanted was peace from the information, and peace from knowing that there were evil-ass bastards in the world, just like the one he was looking at.

The pedophile was at it again, trying to hide pictures and pornography on his computer. Men like him deserved jail, deserved to get the full punishment of the law, and Reed was judge and jury. Reed opened his secure email, linked the attachment of documents, and hit Send, knowing the FBI wouldn't be able to trace the email back to him. He gave the FBI everything they would need to convict the sicko, and all because the man was posting in social media what he had for dinner.

Within ten minutes of meeting his sister-in-law for the first time, he'd known all her secrets. He knew she was adopted, and even had access to the records. Why? Because the government and people lived their lives electronically and online. From social media to their banking accounts. It was all there for his taking, and it drove him nuts, sending him into a lonely existence.

Reed clicked onto his MIA brother, Landon's, Facebook page and scrolled through the pictures. For most, he knew the exact time and place, yet there were a few he'd never seen before. Reed stopped on a photo of the foreign people and places and concentrated.

"I'm going to find you and bring you home." He wasn't trying to spy on his brother, but his entire family was worried about why he was keeping his distance and from Reed's point of view, there was only one way to find out.

Reed's phone rang, pulling him out of his concentration. He swiveled away from the computer and blinked several times so the information boxes would disappear.

He glanced at the caller ID. Unknown Number. Even something as small as a blocked number couldn't be hidden from him.

"Hello."

"Reed." Landon's voice was harsh, and he was out of breath.

"Landon, where the hell have you been, and why are you breathing so heavily?" he asked, as the phone kept cutting in and out.

"I'm in trouble. I sent you a package in the mail, a computer file that's encrypted. I need you to find out what's on it."

"Why didn't you just email it?"

"I just couldn't. You'll understand when you get it."

"Landon, where are you?" Reed asked again, turning to grab a pen from the table. He jotted down the number from the box on a pad before it disappeared.

"I can't tell you. Just decode that file and find Avery."

"Tony's niece? Why would I need to find her?"

"Focus, Reed. You can't tell anyone about this call. Just decrypt the file, find Avery and give her the information. My life depends on it. Do you understand?"

"Of course." Reed bolted out of his chair and turned in circles, spotting the stack of mail sitting on his counter.

"Landon, tell me what's going on." Reed hurried to the stack of mail and flipped through the letters and the packages, not finding anything out of the ordinary. "I haven't received it. When did you send it?"

"Sorry, brother, no time. Tell Avery I'm going underground. She'll know how to find me."

Popping noises and screams in the background had Reed moving the phone away from his ear. When he listened again, he was met with silence.

"Landon, Landon." Reed's worried tone grew louder with intensity. Glancing at the caller ID confirmed his worst nightmare. The phone was dead, and he had no idea where his baby brother was, only that he was in trouble.

Reed picked up the phone countless times to call his other brothers and then set it back down. He searched every piece of mail he had and made an extra trip out to the mailbox, as if what he wanted would magically appear, and still nothing.

"Damn." He threw his remote across the room. The plastic remote put a dent in his drywall before it fell to the ground, cracking into pieces. "Just great." He glanced at his brother's social media page. "Why in the hell couldn't I see your face? I could have had more than just a number."

His gaze landed on the scribbled piece of paper. He snatched it from the counter and slid his chair back to his desk. Reed hacked into the cell provider's database and cell towers to figure out where the signal had originated and to triangulate the location.

Reed frowned and gave a slight shake of his head as he stared at the screen in disbelief. He wasn't on the Island or some big metropolis or, hell, not even in some foreign country like Reed had always assumed. "What in the world are you doing in Riverdale, Texas?"

2 CHAPTER

Reed paced in front of his open living room window with a direct line to the cluster of mailboxes that served his group of townhouses. Glancing over his shoulder, he checked the time again for the hundredth time. "Damn it, what is taking him so long?"

Of all days for the mail to be late, it had to be that day. Every minute that passed was a minute wasted.

Reed stepped outside, darting his gaze up and down the street. There wasn't a single car on the road at that time of day. Not even the mail truck. He fought against a forming headache and plopped down on the stoop, unconsciously picking the leaves from the bush nearby. He tore them to little pieces and dropped them in the flowerbed. His cell phone rang, jolting him from his thoughts. He jumped to his feet and stumbled over the door jamb. He grabbed his phone and checked the caller ID.

All hope fled his body when he recognized the number. "Yeah."

"Now is that any way to answer your phone?" His sister, Skylar, asked in a disapproving tone.

"Today it is. What do you need?" Reed walked back over to the door and leaned on the frame.

"Can't I just call to check on you?"

"No." His answer was short and blunt, maybe a little too blunt. "I'm sorry, Sky, now isn't a good time."

"Is everything okay?"

No, not even close. "Yeah, it's fine. I'm just working on a project and it's...complicated." Reed spotted the mailman and watched as he took his time sorting the mail into the boxes. The urge to buy a cattle prod crossed his mind.

"Reed?"

"Sorry, I'm in the middle of this project. Can I call you back?"

"Sure." He could hear the disappointment in her voice. He knew that tone, the one that made him feel like an ass.

"What did you need?" he asked in a

gentle tone.

"Nothing. It can wait until Sunday at Mom and Dad's house. Go work on your project."

"Are you sure?" he asked, feeling like the lowest form of scum. He ran his hand over his head and squeezed his neck.

"Yeah," she said in a more cheerful tone. "I'll talk to you Sunday, okay?"

"I'm sorry I snapped. It's just this project."

Reed hurried outside with the phone pressed to his ear as he dug out his mail key.

"Really, it's fine. I'll talk to you then. Go kill the virus or whatever has you flustered."

"Okay. Thanks, Sky."

Reed hung up and shoved his key into the mailbox. His stomach turned at what might wait inside. He slowly opened the box and swallowed around the lump in his throat. A manila envelope sat squished inside. "Crap. This isn't happening."

Reed grabbed the envelope, and the rest of the mail, then relocked the box and disappeared back into his townhouse. He tossed the other stuff on the counter and glanced at the package addressed to Scooter Love.

Reed rolled his eyes at the childhood nickname that his brothers used to torment him. Tearing into the envelope,

Reed peered inside. A simple thumb drive lay at the bottom. No note, no directions, nothing but the drive.

He tipped the envelope and caught the thumb drive in his palm. He held it between two fingers and lifted it for a closer look. The drive was covered in tiny holes that looked like small reset buttons on a normal piece of electronic equipment. He'd never seen another one like it. He turned it on its side. The drive was shaped like the letter "L". Instantly the boxes appeared without him even having to insert it into his computer. Numbers, an algorithm, ran like a code meant to be broken or deciphered.

Reed plugged it into his computer and nine boxes appeared on his computer screen and in the pop-up boxes from his ability. In the box that danced next to his computer, the numbers rolled, only stopping on a single digit before moving onto the next in line. Five minutes later, he had all nine numbers, used them like a password and hit enter.

His screen came alive with a ledger similar to a spreadsheet. It listed numbers in one column with corresponding money amounts next to it.

Reed sent the data to his printer before he closed that screen and looked at the next. Pictures of Landon and another man exchanging a briefcase. None of the familiar pop-up boxes appeared as he was studying the new guy. Reed's brows dipped.

"That's weird," he whispered to himself. "Everyone has an online fingerprint. Damn, Lan, what did you get yourself into?"

Reed shoved back from the computer, his mouth parted and his eyes widened as he stared at the last screen. It was a clock counting down with a picture of a skull and crossbones below it with nine more empty boxes where numbers should be.

"Shit." The pop-up box started scrolling through numbers for the combination to fill in the empty boxes as it had done before. The first one stopped, but Reed wasn't watching the numbers as a warning flashed across his screen. Power Down, System Malfunction. Reed's fingers went to work, pulling up every troubleshooting screen to pinpoint the problem. The temperature of his hard drive was heating at an abnormal pace. Reed yanked the thumb drive out of his computer, turning his screen instantly blue. He sat frozen, hoping to hell he hadn't just fried his pride and joy. Anger rippled through his body.

He slowly opened his palm, looking at the drive in a new light. This technology wasn't available on the open market. He shook his head. "Whoever designed this is either a genius or a maniac."

Reed grabbed the papers he'd printed and made another copy, shoving one copy and the thumb drive back into the envelope and stuffing the other one in his backpack. He slid his laptop inside, grabbed some clothes from his dresser, shoved his wallet in his pocket, and grabbed his keys, slamming the door behind him as he left.

He went straight to the bank, opened his safety deposit box and stuck the thumb drive inside, securing it from prying eyes.

Reed parked across the street from Avery's two-story beach home. The windows were open on the second floor, making the curtains dance in the breeze. His sunglasses did little to shield his eyes from the glare of the sun against the white beach sand. He pressed his lips together and rubbed his neck as he tried to figure out how Avery might fit into the picture. A sinking feeling settled in his stomach, and tightness filled his chest. He stepped out of his car and inhaled the salty air as the warmth of the sun heated his skin.

Reed knocked on the door and stepped back, not sure Avery would even remember him. The door swung open, and Reed found himself face to face with a little Italian lady carrying a rolling pin in her hand and with flour on her cheek. The boxes around the woman's head resembled posts on social media feeds. They appeared as if he were looking at computer screen. All the files and information he'd ever need or want were sitting at his finger-tips, and this old lady's boxes contained nothing but an Italian recipe for spaghetti sauce, with unorthodox ingredients, and pictures of her family. The boxes moved with her body, never disappearing from his sight.

"Yes?"

Reed snapped his mouth closed. "Uh hi, I'm Reed Love, and I'm looking for Avery."

The woman took her time replying as she looked him over and glanced at his car across the street. "She's down at the beach." She pulled the door open farther. "You can come through the house."

Reed stepped into the house for the first time. The white, airy home was exactly as he imagined it would be from the road. Tiles covered the floor as light streamed in through the numerous windows, giving him an excellent view of the ocean.

She showed him to the patio door and pointed out into the water. "You'll have to get her attention." She glanced over him again. "That shouldn't be too hard."

Unsure if that was a compliment, or a statement about his casual attire, he stepped outside and walked toward the beach. His shoes sank into the sand as he made his way to the shoreline, where a single towel lay. She was going to think he was crazy. Heck, he wasn't so sure he wasn't.

Reed cupped his hand over his eyes and spotted a surfer in the distance. Not just any surfer but the woman he was looking for. The way she maneuvered her board, staying in front of the breaking wave, left no doubt she knew exactly what she was doing.

When the wave crashed over her and her board popped up before she did, Reed stepped toward the water, only stopping when he spotted her bobbing head. She was looking at him, and her lips were turned down in a frown.

Feeling like an idiot, Reed waved. *I'm such a nerd.*

Avery slid on top of her board and paddled in with the rolling current. When she reached the shallow water, she got off the board, picked it up, and using her free hand, she wiped the water from her face and hair.

Reed forgot to breathe while watching her in a silver screen moment of silence, where the beautiful woman in a tiny bikini rose from the sea. Her curves and long legs....he pushed the thoughts aside. This wasn't the time or the place.

"Close your mouth." She chuckled, slipping her fingers beneath his jaw and pushing it closed. She walked past him and glanced over her shoulder. "And grab my towel, would ya?"

Reed swiped up her towel and shook the sand from it as he followed behind her. "I need your help."

She glanced back again and grinned.

Reed stepped up onto the patio and tossed her the towel after she unhooked the leash from her body. "I'm Reed Love, in case you don't remember me."

"I know who you are," she said, drying her arms and legs. "What I don't know is why you're here in my home."

"Avery Malone, show some manners," the woman Reed assumed was her grandmother called from inside the house.

"Yes, Nonnie." Avery rolled her eyes. "Seems like you made an impression."

"I haven't been here long enough to make an impression."

"Huh." She gestured inside the house. "Come on, Love. You can tell me all about your needs while I change."

Reed swallowed around the lump in his throat as he followed her into the house. She grabbed a water bottle from the fridge and dipped her finger into the pot on the stove, only to get a smack on the ass from the little Italian woman. "You know better than that, child."

"I know, but I couldn't resist." Avery kissed Nonnie on the cheek. "We're going upstairs."

"Good girls don't take men upstairs until they're married."

"Nonnie, it's platonic. Reed is just a friend."

Nonnie pointed the roller at him again. "Why do you only like her as a friend? She's pretty and smart, and she'd make a good wife."

Reed stood speechless until Avery grabbed his hand. "I told you, Nonnie; I'll never be a wife. I've got too much I want to do to settle down."

"You've done enough. It's time, child," Nonnie yelled after them and watched them go up the stairs.

Avery pulled him into her room and shut the door.

"I need your help."

"So you've said," she answered and pulled a pair of silk panties, shorts and a shirt from her dresser. The informational boxes around her head were pictures of exotic locales with one picture of her, Landon, and a small child.

Reed could not look away. His gaze traveled down her body again. His jeans tightened in response. This woman was a walking wet dream. She reached for the straps of her bikini top and tugged. She was about to get naked before his very eyes. He should look away. His manners insisted he turn, so he reluctantly did. He turned away from her and picked up one of the pictures on her dresser.

"Is this you?" he asked, glancing over his shoulder forgetting the reason he'd turned in the first place. She was topless with nothing but shorts covering her body. "Woah, I'm sorry."

She slipped the shirt down over her bare chest. "I'm sure you're no virgin," she answered, moving to stand beside him. "Relax, I don't bite." She smiled. "At least, not on the first date." She chuckled and slid the picture from his hands and replaced it. "You said you needed my help?"

Reed smashed his lips together, warring with exactly what to tell her. "My brother."

She leaned her hip on the dresser. "Which one? You have a handful."

"Landon called me last night. He sounded like he was in trouble, said that he was going underground and that you'd know how to find him."

The playful humor in her eyes began to dim the longer Reed spoke. "Is that all he said?"

"Avery, where's my brother? Why hasn't he come home?"

"I can't tell you much. It's confidential, but I need to know if that's all that your brother said. Why did he call you and not me?"

"What is your connection to him? Please, help me understand."

Avery crossed her arms over her chest. "Reed, you're in way over your head. Just tell me why he called you and then go home. I'll handle it from here."

"I knew this was a bad idea. I should have just called Declan." Reed put his hand on the doorknob, and the next thing he knew he was flung across the room and had landed on her bed; she was straddling his body and pinning his arms down.

"You don't get it, Reed. You aren't leaving this house until I know his exact words and why he called you." She pressed her lips together, and her eyes flickered with heat and determination. "I know a hundred different ways I can hurt you and make you talk, but all you're doing is hindering me from our mutual goal of helping your brother, so start talking."

Reed relaxed in her embrace. The hold on his wrists tightened. "Don't make me pull my knife, sweetie. Just tell me what I need to know."

"Avery, dinner's done. Be a good girl and invite your young man to stay," Nonnie hollered up the stairs.

"Okay, Nonnie, we'll be down in a minute," Avery yelled back. She never removed her gaze from his face. "I have three weapons in this room, all within reaching distance. Start talking, Love."

"He called me because I was the only one that could help him."

"How?"

"He had an encrypted file that he needed me to crack."

"And did you?"

Reed nodded.

"What was on it?"

"Pictures and a ledger."

"Where are they?"

He shook his head. "We find him together, or I don't give them to you."

"Even knowing what I can do to you?"

Reed nodded. "I can help."

"You'll just get in the way."

"You need me, just like Landon does."

"You could die," she said with a straight face.

"So could Landon. I *need* to help you."

Her gaze searched his. Her skin smelled of salt water and was warm like the sun. If they'd been like this for any other reason, he'd flip her and kiss her until she agreed. If he could, and she didn't snap his neck.

Her lips twisted as though she were trying to hide a smile. "You're a good brother."

Reed's brows rose. "That's debatable. A good brother would have found Landon long before now and dragged his sorry butt back."

She leaned down and pressed her lips to his in a quick kiss before she climbed off of him. "Come on. Let's go eat."

This woman was mental. That was the only explanation he could come up with. Reed lifted up on his elbows and watched as she ran her fingers through her wet hair. "Why did you kiss me?"

"Because I wanted to." She turned and waited while he climbed off the bed. "Don't you ever do anything just because you want to?"

Reed shook his head. "No."

"Let's go before Nonnie comes up looking for us with her rolling pin. You do not want to be on the other side of that woman's swing. Trust me."

"What about my brother? I can't just sit down and enjoy a meal."

"Yes, you can. If I know your brother, which I do, then he's already disappeared." She grabbed his hand. "We'll eat, then you'll show me what he sent, and we'll leave first thing in the morning."

Bipolar much? They trampled down the stairs. "You never did tell me how you know my brother."

"We work together," she whispered, walking toward the kitchen. "Now don't be rude; come eat my Nonnie's cooking. It's amazing."

Reed ate, as requested. He complimented Nonnie and hated to admit Avery was right about the food, pushing aside the guilt he should hunt his brother instead of sitting in their company.

Avery walked Reed to his car and she hopped on the hood. "Let's see it."

Reed pulled out the envelope, rested his hip next to her legs, and handed it to her.

"Should we be doing this out in the open?" he asked.

"Sure, it's a nice evening breeze, don't you think?"

"My brother is missing, and you're feeding me pasta and talking about the breeze?"

"Relax, Reed. I'm going to find him," she said, lifting the tab of the envelope. She pulled the documents out a few inches before shoving them back inside.

"Don't you mean we? We're going to find him."

"Yeah. Isn't that what I said?" she asked, hopping down off the car.

"No."

"Hmm. Must have been a slip." She patted his arm and lifted the envelope. "Go get some rest. We're out of here by sunup."

3 CHAPTER

Reed tossed and turned in his bed all night long, unable to get comfortable. They were wasting valuable time. He was up and dressed at 6 AM, before his alarm clock even went off. He had his things packed and ready by the door, waiting. That was what comprised his life, waiting.

When eight o'clock rolled around, and there was still no sign of Avery, deep down in his gut, he knew that he'd been left behind.

"Okay, you want to play games?" Reed mumbled to himself and pulled out his computer chair. "Let's play."

Reed logged into social media and pulled up Avery's page. Just one look at her picture and he'd be able to access whatever the hell he wanted. He started with her bank accounts, looking to see if she'd purchased a plane ticket, and came up empty. He moved to her home and cell phone records, to see if she'd made any calls. Nothing. He pushed away from the computer and stared at it as if it was a foreign object. "I'll find you. I'm not giving up yet."

He spotted the phone number his brother had used to call him and remembered the Texas location. "She had to get off the Island."

Reed grabbed his bag, hopped into his car, and drove back over to Avery's house. He rang the doorbell and could hear someone inside.

Nonnie opened the door. "Yes?"

"I need to talk to Avery, please. We were supposed to meet for coffee."

"She's not here, but she did leave this for you." Nonnie grabbed the same envelope that he'd given Avery yesterday and handed it to him. Reed pulled out the note inside.

I'll bring him back.

"Do you know where she went?"

"I never know with that girl. She's constantly up and leaving in the middle of the night, but come in and let me make you a cup of coffee."

Reed's heart dropped into his stomach.

She'd played him. Leaving in the middle of the night was nearly impossible, especially since neither the ferry nor the airport had flights departing. "Thanks."

Reed followed the woman back into the house, and his gaze darted around, looking for anything that might give him a clue to where or how she'd left.

"How do you like your coffee?"

"Black, please," he answered and slipped onto the bar stool. "She was supposed to come meet my parents today." Reed lied through his teeth.

"Oh." Nonnie's eyes lit with delight. "I'm sure she just forgot. She said she'd only be gone a few days. She mentioned something about surfing before she left for the hangar."

Surfing and the hangar. Now he was getting somewhere. "Do you think you could call her? I'd hate for my parents to set an extra plate if she's not going to be able to make it."

"Sure, dear." Nonnie picked up the phone and Reed watched the number she dialed. He memorized it, surprised to find it wasn't the one she had in her records.

She held out the phone to him as it rang.

"Hey, Nonnie, what's up?" Avery said by way of hello.

"Forget something?" Reed asked, and the line went quiet.

"What are you doing at my house?"

"I was just telling Nonnie that we had plans to meet for coffee, and how disappointed I was that you didn't show up, and now you won't be at our family lunch. My parents are going to be so disappointed."

Nonnie was wiping the counter, as if not listening to their conversation, but he watched the grin on her face.

"Oh....that's just low, Love," she growled into the phone.

"I know. I was really looking forward to our *date*."

"She's standing right there, isn't she?"

He glanced at Nonnie and grinned. "Yep."

"Reed, you know those hundred ways I said I could kill you? I think I've picked just the right one. I'm going to—"

Reed cut her off. "Sure I'll come to you, baby."

"You did *not* just call me baby with her listening."

"Yep, and if you threaten me again, I'll tell her to plan the wedding," he whispered into the phone before raising his voice. "I'll see you soon."

"Reed—"

He hung up on her before she could say anything else.

"Thank you for the coffee, Nonnie, but I'm afraid I've got to run and tell Mom the bad news."

"Anytime, dear." She walked him to the door. "I hope we see you around," she said as a statement instead of a question.

"Me too." He kissed her check and whistled while crossing the street to get back in his car. He pulled out his laptop, used his hot spot to log onto the internet, and pulled up the phone carrier so he could track her location.

Sure enough, the cell was pinging off the same cell towers as his brother's had been.

Reed shut the laptop, grabbed his cell phone, and dialed the one person that could help him.

"Hey, Reed," Reed's brother-in-law, Luke, answered.

"Luke, I need a favor, no questions asked."

"Okay, what do you need?"

"I need to borrow your private jet to fly to Texas, specifically Riverdale, Texas, and I need you to not tell my sister."

"Of course you can borrow the jet, but not telling your sister isn't an option. I don't keep secrets from Sky. Reed, what's going on?"

"Landon is in trouble, and I need to go find him."

"You know this how?"

"It doesn't matter. Can I borrow your jet?"

"Yeah." His answer was hesitant. "Keep it as long as you need. Henry, my pilot, is at your service. Just tell him where you need to go. I'll have him waiting at the hangar."

"Thanks, Luke. I owe you big time. The whole family does."

"Reed. If you need anything else, you call me. I'm not going to tell your sister unless pressed. It might send her into labor, but you call Declan or me. Do you promise?"

"I will. Thanks, Luke."

"And be careful."

"Thanks, can you make that call now? I need to leave as soon as possible."

"Sure. He'll be ready by the time you get there."

Reed hung up and glanced at the page of the ledger he hadn't given Avery. His hold on the steering wheel tightened as he shoved the car into gear and pressed the gas pedal.

****

Reed stepped up to the counter of the B&B in the Riverdale district and glanced around the small establishment. Finding Avery had been a piece of cake when he'd searched all of the area hotels. Just pulling up their websites, with his ability, he had access to their entire database,

28

including their reservation system. This little mom and pop place had been a piece of cake to hack and was in need of stronger security. A quick search of the registered guests, and the dates they'd checked in, and he'd found Avery. Reed signed the registration book and handed over his credit card to the little old lady behind the counter.

"You're smarter than I thought," Avery whispered into his ear.

Reed grinned and glanced over his shoulder. "It wasn't hard, Gidget."

Avery's smile grew wide. "What can I say? I'm a fan of the oldies."

The lady behind the desk slid him back his credit card, and Avery swiped his hotel key from the counter. "Okay, you've proved you can find me. Come on, Love, let's get you settled so we can get to work."

Reed followed Avery up the stairs and into his room. He walked to the window, shifted the curtains, and looked down at the sightseers and tourists below. A group of tables with an array of different colored canopies covered the small street.

"Isn't this a little too out in the open for you?" He dropped the curtain and turned to find Avery relaxing on his bed.

"This is where the action is." She licked her lips.

Reed watched the way she seductively crossed her toned legs on the bed. His mind raced quickly to the gutter. "Uh huh, I'm not falling into your trap. You'll leave me again, only this time tied to the bed." He gestured to her body. "You're a pro at seducing men, aren't you?"

Her lips quivered, and she patted the bed next to her. "I have my moments, but that's not why I'm in your bed." She turned on her side and rested her cheek in her palm. "I've already done recon, and we've got a few hours to kill. It's going to be a long night. I just thought you might like to relax."

Reed leaned against the dresser and crossed his arms over his chest. "What? So you can wait until I fall asleep and stab me with a knife? I don't think so, doll. Where are we going tonight?"

"To a club." She glanced at his bag and slid off the bed. "You did bring more clothes, didn't you?"

She unzipped his bag, not waiting for an invitation and riffled through his clothes. "These won't do."

"What's wrong with jeans?" He grabbed the T-shirt out of her hand, refolded it, and put it back into his bag.

Avery let out a hefty sigh and stood. "Nothing, if we were going to the farm or a bar, but we're not. We're going to need to blend into a place the wealthy use as their playground." She tilted her head. "The man in the picture you gave me is scheduled to attend."

"And he'll know where Landon is?"

"No." She smiled again. "I already know which direction he headed, but in order to help him, we have to figure out why he ran." She slipped a picture out of her pocket and handed it to Reed. "And that man is going to give me answers."

The picture was of a sharply dressed man in a suit, with sunglasses covering his eyes. He was flanked by walls of muscles.

"And how do you plan to get past his bodyguards?"

Avery batted her eyelashes. "I have my ways."

Reed glanced down at the picture again. With all of the training his brother had given him, he might be able to handle one guy, but there was no way in hell he could fight off two.

Reed shook his head. "I don't know..."

"Trust me." She grabbed his arm and the card key and pulled him out of the room. "That's not the security we're going to need to get past." She pulled the door closed behind them. "If you're as good as Landon says you are..."

Reed grabbed her arm, stopping her at the top of the stairs. "What has Landon told you?"

Avery crossed her arms over her chest and tilted her head. "He told me enough.

He told me that you're the best at what you do. He told me about your family and what you're all capable of. What he didn't tell me is how you work; how it is that you were able to decrypt a file that no one could open. You weren't the first one to try and crack those files, but you were the only one that succeeded."

"Who are you?" he asked and stepped back. "And which branch of the government do you work for?"

"None. Your brother and I were recruited by a private organization for our unique assets. Landon, because he can exploit feelings and uses that to help him gain what he needs. Me?" She shrugged. "I'm just good at what I do."

"And what is that?" He narrowed his eyes, wondering just what alternate universe Lan had pulled Reed into.

"Whatever's necessary," she answered and started down the stairs.

"Whatever's necessary to do what?" he asked, grabbing her arm and stopping her again.

"Whatever's necessary to keep your brother alive. He helped me out of a sticky situation once, and I owe him. So if you're done with your questions, we need to go."

Avery started back down the stairs, and Reed followed. He digested the information he'd just learned. Landon trusted this woman since he'd divulged all their family secrets, but the question was, why? Why would he do that and just where was he hiding?

4 CHAPTER

Reed reluctantly followed Avery into Marcello's Suits. At least his inquisition had stopped on the stairs, giving her time to work on her plan for tonight. She knew the layout of the club, and every sordid aspect of the rooms hidden out of sight at the end of the hall. Even the most prepared operative would have a hard time alone, and here she was with a tagalong.

"Ah, Marcello," Avery whispered while being kissed on both cheeks by the tiny man.

"Avery. What a pleasant surprise."

"My friend here needs a new look."

"Hey, what's wrong with my look?" Reed asked.

"Humor me." Avery glanced over her shoulder and lifted her brow before returning her attention to Marcello. "I want arm candy, so he needs to look sharp, sexy, wealthy, and mouth watering."

"You don't ask for much." Marcello moved around Reed, pushing his arms out to his side to get a better look.

He glanced between Reed and her. "Tonight? Avery, dear, I'm good, but I'm not that good. That's not a lot of notice."

"I know, and you know I wouldn't ask if it wasn't important."

Marcello quirked his brow. "You're related to Landon? Same physique, bone structure, and those eyes." Marcello sighed.

"You know my brother?"

"Of course," Marcello answered. "I'm the best in town for what he orders."

Reed jerked his gaze to Avery and lifted his brow.

"Do you happen to have any of Landon's suits you were holding? They're about the same size."

Marcello rested his finger on his chin as he glanced at Reed once more. "It just so happens I do. He wasn't in to pick up his last order." He glanced at Avery. "Will he need the full workup?"

Avery nodded. "Yes. Unfortunately, this isn't a casual visit. It's work related.

We'll need all the bells and whistles."

Marcello nodded. He knew exactly what she meant. Explaining it to Reed might be more difficult. "Show him to the room and have him change."

"You're a doll." She kissed Marcello's cheek and took Reed's hand, slipping her fingers through his. She showed him into the dressing room and then stepped in behind him, locking the door.

"Do you normally help men dress?" His lips quirked.

"Only when they need it." She wiggled her brows and squeezed his fingers before pulling on the hanging hook next to the mirror. Reed's eyes widened, and his mouth parted. She held her grin, watching Reed's expression. She didn't get to share the perks of her world with many people, so this one little moment in time was a small treat.

"Unbelievable." Reed stepped into the hidden room. Guns hung on the racks covering the walls. Landon's black Armani suit hung on a mannequin in the back room, in front of three mirrors. Sophisticated and mouth-watering. Reed, in that suit, would be both of those things and so much more. Reed turned in a circle and let out a low whistle. "Landon is like Bond, isn't he?"

"He hates playing dress-up." Avery walked over to the mannequin. "Your brother is really down to earth. It took a lot of convincing to get him on board with the company's agenda."

"And what agenda is that?"

Avery stopped unbuttoning the pants and looked up at him, glad she wasn't with Landon's other brother, the human lie detector.

"Has your brother ever told you how we met?"

"No, and you're changing the subject."

"Of course I am." She shrugged. "I'd seen him on our Island, but I didn't know him well. I didn't know many of your family well. I'm afraid my job keeps me away from home a lot. So you can imagine my surprise when I bumped into him in the back alleyway of a hotel in South America." She returned to working the clothes off the mannequin. "He was special ops then, tracking a drug lord. Anyway, we were in a little town in the middle of the jungle. The place was primitive at best. No clean running water, no medical services, not much of anything except this little dive of a hotel and a local watering hole for drunks."

"What were you doing there?"

"Your brother lost his entire team on that mission, and he'd been shot. Someone inside the agency sold them out, and when he stumbled into the alley at that exact moment, it seemed that fate had to have guided him that day."

Reed shrugged out of his T-shirt and slipped into the crisp white shirt. "You don't strike me much as a person who believes in fate."

"I don't, but he does." Her gut clenched as she remembered the defeat in Landon's eyes, the pain, not from his injury but from his loss.

"What happened to Landon?"

"I saved him. I aborted the reason I was there, and I called in a rescue. My company"—she cleared her throat and handed the pants to Reed—"came in and took us both out. I got reprimanded for it, but saving Landon's life was the right thing to do. What was I going to do, let him die?"

Reed kicked off his shoes, unbuttoned his jeans, and slid them off. She took her time looking her fill while he changed into the pants. Reed was a briefs man, not those tighty whities but black biker briefs, and the package he teased her with...She lifted her gaze, trying not to look impressed and hungry.

"I thought you said that he saved your life."

"He did." She spun around and grabbed the dress shoes. "He's been there for me more times than I care to admit, and saved me in other ways." She handed him the dress shoes.

Reed sat down on the pillar in front of the mirrors and looked up at her, with the shoes still in his hand. Was that pity in his eyes? Did he even understand what she was telling him?

"Landon and you?" He searched her eyes for answers she wasn't ready to explain.

She sat down next to him. "Landon," she started and then stopped, swallowing around the lump in her throat. "Lan gets me. He can read me, and I'm not talking about his ability. I went through a rough time, and he was there for me."

Reed dropped his gaze to the shoes. "So my brother and you? You're what? An item?"

"No," she said, rising from her seat. "With my work, I don't have time for relationships, but Landon and I are really good friends." She shook her head. "He's not just my good friend. He's my best friend."

"You aren't a couple?"

"No."

Reed dropped the shoes and stood, closing the distance between them. He cupped her cheek and held her gaze. "Then he won't mind that I do this."

Reed ran his thumb over her bottom lip as he lowered his mouth to hers in a kiss that surprised her. His lips were soft, and she opened for him, letting him in to plunder her mouth. He tasted of mints and coffee as he held her tight against his length. He tested, and she took. His palm rested on the small of her back, his fingers teasing the waistband of her jeans. She toyed with running her fingers over the crisp white shirt, wishing for a moment he didn't have it on.

"You two should get a room, and I don't mean this one," Marcello said as he crossed the room.

"You're just full of surprises, Love. That was bold."

"I have no doubt you could have, and would have, stopped me if you wanted."

"You're right." She smiled. "Why did you kiss me?" she whispered against his lips.

"Because I wanted to." Reed winked as he dropped his hold and stepped back, resuming his seat to try on the shoes.

"Do we need any alterations?"

"No," Reed said, sliding his foot in the second shoe. "It fits like a glove."

Avery grabbed the jacket and held it out to him to slide into. Marcello crossed his arm over his chest. Resting his elbow on his arm, he played with the scruff on his chin. "It'll do."

Damn, if that wasn't an understatement. Reed was hot dressed to the nines. He could easily fit in with the men at the club, and if Avery didn't have her own agenda, she'd be spending half the night fighting off the cougars in search of new blood. She might have told Reed he was her arm candy, but the truth was, he was a four-course meal with a side of dessert to a starving woman on a diet. Good God, all the Love boys sure knew how to fill out a suit, but Reed....just damn.

"It'll do."

Marcello moved to Avery's side as they watched Reed turn toward the mirrors.

"Wipe your chin, darling," he whispered as he leaned in to kiss her cheek. "He's delicious, and I want details."

Avery chuckled before stepping around him and taking one of the guns off the wall while Reed changed out of his clothes and put his jeans on again. "Put this on my tab."

"You got it, doll. I have the bullets in the case, and I'll put them in the shoe box."

Avery popped the magazine clip out to make sure it wasn't loaded before shoving the gun into the waistband beneath her shirt.

"How did you get here so fast, Reed?"

"Luke's jet," he answered, slipping back into his shoes.

"Is the jet still here?" She turned to find him redressed.

"Yeah, why?"

"Have it on standby tonight. We aren't staying."

"What about our stuff?"

"I'll have everything taken care of. You just call Henry and tell him to be fueled and waiting."

"Should I even ask you how you knew the pilot's name?"

She smiled but didn't answer. "I'll take care of everything, just have him ready. Wheels up at midnight."

"Like Cinderella leaving the ball?"

"If Cinderella carries a gun and has to crack some heads, then sure."

"I'm going to kill Landon."

"Not if I do it first."

The look Reed gave her, as though deciding if she was serious, was priceless.

5 CHAPTER

Five hours later, Reed pulled at the hem of his suit jacket one more time, and stepped out of the Town Car driven by someone Avery introduced as Sam. Sam looked as though he could easily have been drafted as a linebacker for a professional football team. The restaurant in front of them looked nice, but he felt extremely overdressed for the ribs and chicken they advertised on their sign. He pointed to a man as he passed into the restaurant. "Hey, he's wearing jeans."

"Quit being a baby." She grinned. "We aren't here for dinner."

"How long have you known Sam?" Reed asked.

"Long enough," she said, moving to stand in front of him. "Sam will be waiting for our exit."

"Okay." Reed tugged at his red tie to loosen it.

"Quit fidgeting. You look great." She slid her red clutch beneath her arm and straightened his tie as he watched. He stilled his fingers from touching her, as he had done when she'd changed for the night. His mouth had watered when she'd stepped out in the short red dress that hugged every curve. When she'd turned, and he'd glimpsed the back, his body responded. The backless dress made every nerve in his body stand at attention. His fingers itched to touch the smooth skin.

"Just stick by my side and we'll get through this unscathed. We get in, get what we need, and get out. Simple."

"Right, simple. Remind me again why we're doing this. Why we can't just leave and find my brother?"

"Your brother was looking for intel on someone who didn't want to be found."

"Who?" he asked.

Avery ran her hands up his jacket and around his neck, lowering his head to kiss him. Not that he minded. He pulled her closer and held on to her until Avery broke away. She glanced over her shoulder at the couple that had passed, talking in hushed tones.

"You ask a lot of questions."

"And you aren't giving me answers."

"Strictly need to know." She patted his jacket before running the pad of her thumb over his lips. "Just follow my lead."

Avery slipped her fingers around the crook of his arm, bypassed the door to the restaurant, and rounded the corner into the alleyway.

"Uh...are we going in through the kitchen?" He gestured with his thumb, pointing back the way they had come.

"We're going to the underground," she whispered. Her stilettos clicked against the pavement. The smell of stale food drifted to his nose from the dumpster they had passed. If this was where the wealthy hung out, they needed a new realtor. The alleyway was littered with cans and newspapers as she led him farther into the dark. She paused at a doorway with a keypad on the abandoned building next door. Quick to press buttons, he heard the door click, and she yanked it open.

Light spilled out as he stepped inside and paused. Her hand on his arm tightened as she leaned into him. "Just relax."

"What is this place?" he asked as another couple entered and stepped around them to the only desk in the lobby.

The woman's dress ended at the top of her thighs. Her thigh-high boots were black and shiny. The woman glanced over her shoulder and winked in Reed's direction as the man with her talked with the receptionist. Each one of them had pop-up boxes with information around them. Each an invitation, if he wanted to actually find out who they were.

The receptionist greeted them in hushed tones before disappearing with the couple behind another secure door.

Avery turned toward him and straightened his tie again. "This is an exclusive club."

"What kind of club?"

"Relax," she whispered when the receptionist returned. Avery slipped her fingers through his and guided him to the desk.

The blonde receptionist smiled as they approached.

"Avery Malone."

The woman nodded. "Of course, Ms. Malone, a party for four. It's a pleasure to see you again."

"Thank you, Angelica. Is Mr. Franklin here yet?"

Angelica's boxes popped up the minute they'd walked into the door. Pictures of her in a flowered dress on a beach with a fruity umbrella drink in her hand filled one of her boxes. The smile on her face was genuine as she looked up into the eyes of the man plastered to her side. Dark sunglasses covered his eyes as he looked down at this woman.

Angelica moved to the keypad on the door and punched in numbers. "Mr. Franklin is already seated. If you'll just follow me."

She held the door open for them to step inside, and they waited for her to lead the way into the dim room. Soft music drifted to his ears as they passed tables of well-dressed people sitting and speaking in hushed tones. Couples and groups were sitting together in the semi-circular booths. A woman was kissing a man with another woman on his side, and she was rubbing his chest. Exactly what type of club had Avery dragged him into?

The man in the booth broke the kiss, turned to the other woman, and kissed her. Avery's grip on Reed's arm tightened and pulled him to walk again.

Angelica stopped in front of a booth in the corner away from the others, which was guarded by two beefy men wearing sunglasses and suits. She held out her hand, gesturing to the table. "Ms. Malone has arrived," she informed the guards, who stepped aside and let them pass. Angelica lowered her eyes, and her cheeks turned pink as she smiled at the man in the booth.

The man slid out of the booth and rose. "Avery. It's a pleasure."

He leaned into her and kissed both of her cheeks.

"Stuart," she breathed between them before returning to Reed's side. "I'd like you to meet Reed Love. Reed, this is Stuart Franklin."

Reed's jaw clenched as he realized he was being introduced to the man in the pictures, the one who was passing the briefcase. It was the same man in Angelica's picture.

Reed shook Stuart's hand. His grip was strong as he squeezed, and Reed squeezed back. Stuart's lips twitched before he dropped his hold and gestured to the booth.

"And this is my lovely companion tonight, Emily Page."

"Pleasure." The woman smiled up at them. "Please join us."

The atmosphere in the room was thick with secrecy and tension as they slid into the booth.

"You took a risk coming here with him," Stuart was quick to say.

Avery rested her palm on Reed's leg. "I trust him."

Stuart glanced between the two. "That speaks volumes, but unfortunately, I don't have that luxury." He slid out of the booth and held out his palm for Emily. "Emily, be a doll and take Mr. Love to the dance floor."

Emily slipped out of the booth and smiled. "Mr. Love, would you care to dance?"

Reed glanced at Avery, who gave a little nod. "Of course he would, but first..."

"Avery..."

Avery leaned in and pressed her lips to his, killing the question on his lips. Her soft body melded into his as she wound her fingers around his neck and tilted her head, deepening their kiss. Her tongue dueled with his in a dance that made it difficult to remember exactly why they were there. Her taste, her touch, ignited a fire that was hard to tame. She pulled free, her eyes glazed as she looked into his eyes. His breath came out in pants as her fingers slid farther up his thigh with unspoken promises.

"It's not polite to make a lady wait." Her lips twisted into a smile at her sexual innuendo.

"I'll remember that." He winked and slid out of the booth, placing his palm on Emily's back and leading her to the occupied dance floor.

Reed rested his palm on Emily's hips as they swayed on the dance floor to the slow song. Emily seductively pressed into him, and even that wasn't enough for Reed to take his gaze off Avery.

"She was staking her claim."

Reed glanced at the redhead in his arms. "Excuse me?"

"Avery. She was letting me know that you're off-limits."

"What? Is a hot kiss some type of girl code?"

Emily rested her hands on his neck as she glanced back at the table. "Yes. I've known Avery a long time."

"How do you know her?" Reed turned the woman so he could keep an easier eye on the table. The boxes around Emily were easy to read. Her pictures weren't anything to brag about, her bank account far less interesting, even if this woman was living comfortably. He studied her playful expression, the way her eyes sparkled with mischief.

"Through work. The same way I know your brother, although I must say, you're a much better dancer than he is."

That statement caught him off guard, and he stilled their movement.

Her hands moved to his and squeezed. "Keep dancing."

Reed moved slower. "I seem to be at a disadvantage. Everyone I've met knows my brother, yet I don't know anyone."

Reed nodded toward the table. "What's Stuart's story? Does he work with Avery and you also?"

"Oh no." She grinned, and he spun

them around again. "He's one of the most vile, arrogant men you'll ever meet."

A shiver skirted down her spine, and Reed pulled her closer and turned them again. "Why are you with him?"

"The same reason Avery is here." She smiled and ran her hands up into Reed's hair. "For information."

"What's your connection? Who was Landon looking for?"

Her smile faltered, and Reed maneuvered them through the throng of people to the other side of the room, even farther away from the table.

She looked up into his eyes. "He was looking for my sister."

"I don't understand." Reed took her hand and led her toward a hallway, away from prying eyes and ears.

"And I don't have time to explain." She glanced nervously up the hallway before pulling him toward the other end. She opened a door at the end of the hall and shoved him inside, following behind. She flicked the lock and turned on the light. A bed with red satin sheets sat in the middle of the room with little else but the cuffs and chains dangling on the side.

"My sister went missing six months ago," she said, slipping a strap off her shoulder. Reed stepped back and held up his hands.

"Listen, I don't know what this place

is, but..."

Emily rolled her eyes and closed the distance between them. She reached for his tie and loosened it before taking the clip out of her hair, letting the loose curls run down her back. "This is a gentleman's club." She gestured to the bed. "It's exactly what it looks like." She loosened his tie and started unbuttoning his shirt.

"What are you doing?" he asked, placing his fingers over hers, stilling her greedy hands.

"Making this look believable," she answered. "As I was saying, my sister, Alice, went missing six months ago from her home."

Emily leaned into kiss his neck, and Reed's hold on her arms tightened.

"Work with me. They'll come looking for us in a minute, and we're running out of time." She brushed his hands away and kissed the other side of his neck before she moved him back to the bed and pushed him to sit. "Alice is a doctor, and when she didn't show up for rounds, they called me. I went to her house and it was a mess. There was blood everywhere, and the place was trashed. Her medical bag was missing, and there were syringes and cotton pads soaked in blood left by the bed. I knew something bad had happened, but I had no idea what, so I called Landon for help."

Emily climbed onto the bed, lifted her dress up to her thighs, and straddled his waist, pushing Reed to lie down.

"Landon must have gotten too close to uncovering the truth." She leaned down over him and pressed a quick kiss on his lips. "He found that Stuart had been watching her. He might have had something to do with her disappearance. That's why I'm with him. He knows what happened."

"Did you ask him?"

"God, no," she whispered. "Landon paid for the information."

"The briefcase," Reed whispered.

"Stuart had one condition."

Reed's brows dipped, and his stomach churned, as he hesitated, not sure he wanted to know what that information might be.

"He wanted me in exchange for the information."

"Why?" Reed leaned up on his elbows. "He's holding you as what? A prisoner?"

"I'm his bargaining chip that she won't go to the police. He acts like he knows where Landon is holed up, and I'd give my bank account that he knows where Alice is being held." She leaned down, and her body stiffened, her breath hot against his lips. "I'm so sorry," she whispered before pressing her lips to his.

A second later, the door was kicked in.

Stuart walked in with his bodyguards, and Avery stepped in behind them.

Emily gasped as she was yanked off of Reed. Stuart's eyes were narrowed, and the grip on Emily's arm turned white around Stuart's fingers. "Did you forget your place?"

Emily's eyes widened in horror as he passed her off to his guards.

Reed slid off the bed and held Avery's hurt-filled gaze. She didn't speak.

"Avery, I didn't know you liked to share your toys," Stuart insinuated and slid up behind her. He wrapped his arms around her waist as they both held Reed's gaze. "I think it's only fair I return the favor."

Avery clenched her eyes closed as Stuart pressed his lips to her neck, letting his mouth linger around his smile, almost daring Reed to try something.

Reed stepped closer, and Avery held up her hand.

Stuart moved to the other side of her neck and placed another kiss as his hand slid up her waist to right below her breast.

"Nice of Emily to leave a trail of lipstick showing where she's been."

"Stuart, I kissed him," Emily said, and one of the guards started to drag her out of the room.

Stuart held up his hand and released Avery, turning to Emily. He lifted his hand to smack her, and an anger Reed rarely felt bubbled up inside his veins. He grabbed Stuart's hand, stopping him before he made contact.

"I kissed her, and I would have fucked her, if we hadn't been interrupted."

Stuart yanked his hand free, and Reed never saw the fist that connected with his face, knocking him to the ground. He cupped his aching jaw when Stuart's foot connected to his ribs, leaving Reed gasping for air.

Reed glanced up to find Avery being held back, venom in her eyes.

Stuart slid a gun out of the waist of his dress pants and bent down, pressing the silencer of the gun against Reed's head. "Someone needs to teach you some manners."

Reed swallowed around the lump in his throat and brushed his fingers against the blood on his lip. "You call a sucker punch teaching me manners?"

Reed spit out the blood before he felt another blow to the side of his face. He collapsed on the floor, and his world turned dark.

6 CHAPTER

"Now we're even," Stuart said, glaring down at Reed.

Avery yanked out of the beefy arms holding hers, struggling to get to the gun before it went off. Stuart had already knocked Reed out, and now Reed's shoulder oozed with blood. Avery's heart raced as she pushed her way between the gun and Reed, blocking any more shots. She pulled the knife from the sheath beneath her dress and held it against Stuart's crotch. "Touch him again and I'll cut off your balls and shove them down your throat."

Stuart's nostrils flared, and Avery held his glare and slowed her breathing, holding the knife in place. "Those are big words for a little girl. Do you think you can beat my guards and me all by yourself?"

"She doesn't need to." Sam's deep voice was a relief to her ears as he and another agent, Rick, stepped into the room with guns pointed at the two bodyguards.

"You okay?" Rick asked.

She nodded but refused to look away from Stuart as she slipped the gun free from his fingers. She cold-cocked him with the butt of the gun, returning the favor he'd done to Reed. Stuart dropped to the floor unconscious. She lifted the gun and aimed it at the asshole as venom coursed through her veins. She pulled the trigger, making an identical hole in his shoulder as he'd done to Reed. "*Now* we're even."

Sam and Rick held the bodyguards at gunpoint and disarmed them before gesturing with the barrel of their guns for them to sit on the bed. Avery helped Emily restrain them with the cuffs and chains attached to the bed, the kinky shit coming in handy for once.

"You put Reed in danger," Avery gritted out through clenched teeth without looking up at Emily.

"I didn't have a choice." She clicked the cuffs in place and stood. "They know where Landon is hiding. I had to make my move; it was either now or never."

Avery shook her head, moved to Reed's side, and lifted him to look at the exit wound on his back. The bullet had made a clean shot, in one side and out the other.

"We need to get Reed out of here." She glanced up at Sam, and Rick and he shoved their guns away and moved her out of the way. Sam handed his gun to Emily before lifting Reed to carry him out fireman style. Avery and Emily took up the rear, watching behind them in the event they were followed.

Sam had the SUV just outside the exit door and hurried to lay Reed inside as the others got in. Sam slid behind the wheel. Rick had his phone pressed to his ear. "Send the maid. We need a cleaning."

Code words for someone to come clean up the mess they'd left behind. Within ten minutes of the call, someone would come to take care of the Stuart and the guards, holding them in containment to extract information.

****

Reed relaxed into the soft bed and turned his head toward the warmth of the light. He'd dreamt of Avery in her short dress, and within seconds, the memories came flooding back. His eyes shot open.

The room he was in wasn't the B&B where they were staying. His jaw ached, and he reached for it, stopping short at the pull in his arm. He glanced to his side and found an IV hanging. A line attached from a drip bag ran to his arm.

Reed reached for the bandage on his shoulder and winced from his touch.

"Where am I?"

"You shouldn't move." Emily's voice drifted to his ears as she rose from the seat across the room and approached the bed. "You're in a safe house outside of town."

"You?" Reed snarled.

Emily lifted her hands and froze in her spot. "You were shot."

Reed's brows dipped as he tried to remember being shot. He didn't.

"Where's Avery?"

"She stepped out to talk to Sam and Rick. She'll be right back."

"How long have I been out?"

"Two days."

Reed let out a resigned breath before he remembered what Emily had said in the room, before the door busted in at the gentleman's club.

"They found Landon. I've got to help him." He moved to sit up and reached for the IV in his arm. Emily was by his side within seconds, trying to hold him down.

"Avery," she hollered. "Landon is safe for now."

Reed abandoned his efforts to get up.

"But you said..."

"Stuart is a little tied up, not to mention sporting the same wound as you."

Reed shook his head, trying to make sense out of Emily's words. "He was shot?"

Emily's lips twisted at the corners as she moved from the bed when Reed relaxed. "You can thank your girlfriend for that. She must really like you."

The door flew open and Avery stood on the threshold. "Nice of you to rejoin us, Love," she said as she stepped into the room. "You gave us a little scare."

Avery glanced at Emily and nodded toward the door.

"Let me know if you need anything." She gave Reed a small smile. "I am so sorry for what happened."

Reed waited for the door to close. "What exactly happened? She said I was shot."

"You were. Stuart knocked you out cold and then shot you. Luckily, he only got your shoulder."

"And you returned the favor?"

Avery's cheeks turned a light shade of pink. The look was unfamiliar and turned him rock hard in seconds. Avery blushing was a sight, and he quietly wondered how he might be able to make her do it again. "He's lucky I didn't cut off his balls first."

"Ouch."

Avery crawled up next to him on the

bed and rested her cheek in her palm as she held his gaze, reading him like an open book.

"Those things I said in the room..."

Avery's lips tilted up in the corners. "You mean when you took the blame for kissing Emily, and how you were going to screw her."

Reed swallowed. "Yeah...that."

"I know why you said it. Stupid, but I understand." She cupped his cheek. The warmth of her touch was familiar and gentle. She leaned in and pressed a soft kiss to his lips. "If you ever do anything like that again, I'll personally beat more sense into that thick skull."

"Emily said Stuart knew where Landon was. We have to find him before he gets himself killed, Avery."

Avery rolled to lie on her back and stared up at the ceiling. "I sent a team in to extract Landon. They checked where I thought he'd be hiding, but he was gone."

"Emily said Landon was looking for her sister, Alice. Maybe he found her, and they're on the run."

Avery shook her head, reached for Reed's hand, and laced their fingers together. "Stuart sent Landon into a trap, set up by the people who have Alice."

Air in Reed's lungs rushed out, his shoulders tightened, and he closed his eyes. "How do you know that?"

"My employer has a way of getting people to talk."

Reed turned to meet her gaze. "What if Landon's hurt or, God forbid, captured?"

"He's not. Landon got out."

"You don't know that."

She turned to face him again. "Yes, I do." She gave him a small smile. "The first day I started working with Landon, we set up a code that only he and I know."

Reed frowned, trying to push back the hope that bloomed in his chest.

"What kind of code?"

"An ad in the *New York Chronicle*."

Avery slipped out of the bed and crossed the room, returning moments later with a paper in her hand. She read. "Sexy man wanted, must love long walks on the beach." She grinned and glanced at him before continuing. "Must be sensitive and caring." Her sultry voice lowered as she continued. "Only surfers need apply."

"And he'll know that's you?"

"Yeah, and the series of x's and o's I included at the end will tell him exactly where to find me and when to meet. He checks the paper daily and knows that when he sees that ad, he's to drop everything and meet at our designated rendezvous spot, no matter what he's involved with."

"What if he can't?"

"He will." She leaned down and kissed

his lips again. "He's already responded."

"What? How? Did he call?"

Avery's eyes softened, and she twisted the ad section around so he could see. She pointed to another ad in the paper. *Surf's up, Gidget.*

"Get some rest while I make you something to eat. We're leaving in twenty-four hours for the rendezvous point."

7 CHAPTER

Avery stopped Sam in the hall. Having an ex-military medic on the team was a must in her line of work. "How is he?"

"A little sore from the stitches, but it's to be expected. The wound looks good, so that's always a bonus. I removed the IV, so he's mobile; just keep an eye on him and the bandage."

The tension in Avery's shoulders released. Losing Reed wasn't an option, and not just because Landon would kill her. In the short time she'd spent with Reed, he'd found a way into her thoughts, digging beneath the walls she kept firmly in place. "Thanks."

Avery walked into the empty room and stilled. The sound of running water drifted to her ears so she moved to the open bathroom door and leaned against the wall facing the bedroom window. "Reed, are you okay?"

"I wish everyone would quit asking me that."

Avery's lips twisted into a smile, and the clench in her chest released like a breath of fresh air. "What are you doing?"

"I saw you got my bags, so I'm taking a bath and changing clothes."

"Are you decent?"

There was a splashing sound. "Damn it."

Avery pushed off the wall and looked into the bathroom. Reed was already in the tub trying to grab and open the shampoo bottle with one hand. The spa-sized tub kept most of him out of her view. "Can I give you a hand?"

"Is that a loaded question?" he asked, and his grin turned mischievous.

"Get your mind out of the gutter. I'm talking about with your hair."

Avery flipped a switch, and the jets in the tub started, creating bubbles, and giving him cover.

"Oh, now that feels good." He rested his head against the wall.

Avery stripped to her panties and bra, grabbed a towel and rolled it up, putting it under Reed's arm on the side of the tub to help stabilize the movements. She gestured for Reed to move forward before she climbed in behind him. She gently guided his head back into the water, holding him from going under before she helped him to sit up. Within minutes, she had his hair washed with little complaint. Avery had risen to get out when Reed stopped her.

"Aren't you going to wash my back too?"

"You're pushing it, Love."

"You know you want to," he teased.

Avery eased back down into the warm water, picked up the soap, and lathered the suds in her hands before resting her palms on his body. Her body heated from the tiny contact, making her long for things she hadn't realized she'd been missing.

"Do you come here often?" Reed teased.

"You're such a nerd. Is that the best you've got?"

"Not by a long shot." He chuckled when his hand landed on her leg. She ignored the connection and worked knots out of his back, careful of the bandage on his shoulder.

"Oh, that feels good." Reed moaned, and his fingers traveled a path behind his back following the curve of her leg up to the juncture of her thighs.

Her fingers stilled, and she leaned her

head against his back and closed her eyes. "I guess you never learned the lesson in school about keeping your hands to yourself."

"I must have missed that day."

"Obviously."

Reed ran his fingers over the wet fabric covering her mound, teasing her.

"This would be a lot easier if we changed places." He glanced over his shoulder and she leaned in so he could capture her lips. He rubbed harder. His fingers toyed with the elastic of her panties, and there was nothing she wanted more.

Avery rose and slid around him to stand in front of him. Reed had his hand on her leg and rubbed it up her thigh.

"You're wearing too many clothes." He leaned forward and kissed her leg, His hand traveled up the back of her leg to her ass. "Take them off, Avery."

"For someone with an injury, you're awfully demanding." Avery reached behind her and unhooked her bra, letting it slip down her arms. She tossed it onto the bathroom floor.

"A brush with death will do that to a man." He rubbed her leg again. "Damn, you're beautiful. Come closer."

Avery wiggled her pointer finger and reached for her panties, slowly sliding those down her legs. She stepped out of those, too, and tossed them over the side of the tub. She eased down into the water. His palm rested on her waist as she took his length in her hand and stroked him once before she eased his erection inside her. His girth touched every part of her, deliciously stretching her to accommodate his size.

Reed moaned, and his hand tightened on her hip as he leaned forward and took her breast into his mouth, toying with her nipple and sending an electric current straight to her core. Reed moved to the other one, running his tongue over her breast and scraping his teeth against her skin.

"I don't do relationships," she whispered and eased back down on him.

"We'll change that," he answered, pistoning his hips up to fill her completely. She held his hooded gaze and lifted up before sliding back down, increasing her movements with the need that filled her.

"No, we won't," she said on a breath. She moaned. "God, you feel so good."

"Wait until I'm in control." He kissed her chest. Water sloshed around the tub from their frenzied movements.

"You need to go back home and let me handle this."

Reed lifted his hips again, meeting her on the down stroke. "Not a chance."

"It's dangerous." Her words came out

on a pant. Every nerve fiber in her body was strung tight as she built closer to the edge of her orgasm.

"I should have asked earlier. Are you on the pill?" Reed asked, slipping his fingers between them and circling her clit; the added stimulus had her channel tightening around his shaft as she fought the release.

"Yeah, and you're changing the subject."

"I learned from the master." He kissed her hard. "I'm not sure I could have stopped if you'd said no." He held her gaze. The heat in his eyes matched the intensity of the warmth coursing through her body.

"Come for me, baby. I'm not going to last," Reed whispered and quickened the circle over her tiny bud.

"No." She kept moving, fighting harder not to come. "You first."

"Together." He pressed down on her clit and lifted his hips harder.

Avery's body tightened when her orgasm hit. Her movement stilled as she held on to him, savoring every spasm that wrung through her. Reed moaned her name, lifting his hips and spilling his seed. He moved his hand to her waist and held her to keep the connection.

She lowered her head to his good shoulder until she caught her breath. "We shouldn't have done that."

"We should have been doing that the entire time."

"Reed, I don't need a fuck buddy, and that's all you'd be." Avery eased off of him and stood to climb out of the water. "I was serious about you going home."

Reed wobbled to stand, knocking the towel to the floor. "Then you should know I was serious when I said that I'm not going anywhere."

Avery grabbed a towel from beneath the sink and dried her face and her chest. "You're hurt. You're no good to anyone."

"I think I just proved that theory wrong." Reed stepped out of the tub, and she grabbed his towel and tossed it at him.

"I don't need any emotional ties." She turned to leave, and he stopped her, pressing her against the door, and their eyes met.

"Nice to see you're not emotional and clingy." He smiled and watched her throat contract as it swallowed. "The woman I know doesn't run from anything."

"Shows you exactly how much you don't know about me. I don't stick around...for anyone." Her eyes searched the depths of his baby blues, hoping that the resolve showed on her face. She was falling for this Love, and in her line of work, that had disaster written in bold.

The first thing they'd taught her in the academy was to find her own weaknesses and come to grips with the possibilities of them being exploited. Avery had that narrowed down to one, Nonnie, and there was no way in hell she was about to make that two. Landon was close enough to being the second, and even he was a risk she hadn't wanted to take.

"Consider me warned." He cupped her cheek and thoroughly kissed her until her body melded against his before he pulled away. "Unless you want me to take you again, I suggest you get dressed."

He tapped her on the ass and moved out of the doorway and into the room, where he struggled one-handed with the zipper on his bag and getting his clothes out.

"Reed, we should talk."

"No need," he said, sitting on the bed, trying to maneuver his track pants up his legs. "I heard you loud and clear." He rose and pulled the pants up to his waist. "You don't do relationships. That's your right."

He grabbed a T-shirt out of his bag and slid it up his bandaged arm before twisting to get it over the rest of his body. "My right is to try and convince you otherwise."

"Reed, you're wasting your time." She tossed her towel at him before stomping over to her bag and yanking out her clothes. The man infuriated her. The ending would be the same, no matter what tactics he tried to implement.

"It's my time to waste." With a smile on his lips, Reed watched her dress.

"I'm not going to fall for you." She glanced at him as she pulled up her panties and jeans. "I'm not the falling type. You picked the wrong girl." Her words were ice cold, and her resolve just as frozen. She wouldn't give him an inch, no matter what her body and her heart wanted. Not now, not ever.

"I heard you, princess."

Princess? He did *not* just call her princess. She snapped her gaze to his and bit the inside of her cheek, trying to hold back a snappy retort that was at the tip of her tongue. "Reed, you're a nice guy."

"I don't want to be nice. They finish last."

"You'll find a girl back home that wants to spend time with you, one that will swoon and fall at your feet. One that's looking for a serious relationship." The words left a sour taste in her mouth, but she pushed through. "And when you do, you'll fall madly in love and live your happily ever after." She pulled her shirt on and straightened her shoulders. "I'm happy with my life just the way it is. It's easier this way."

He gave a little nod, grabbed his

backpack, and slung it over his good shoulder. "You don't have to beat a dead horse, Avery. I heard you loud and clear; let's call a truce. Agree to disagree. You'll come around. I think you just need more time to admit that we'd be good together." He glanced up at her. "In and out of bed."

She'd never admit it, even if there was a smidgen of truth to his words.

8 CHAPTER

After dinner, Avery stood on the back patio with a coffee cup in hand as she watched the moon dip below the horizon. She sipped her coffee, letting the warmth spread down her throat and into her system. She'd almost lost Reed, and knew damn well it was due to the danger she'd led him into.

"Don't beat yourself up. Reed's going to be fine," Emily said, closing the door behind her. "He's a tough guy, just like his brother."

Avery shook her head. "He's nothing like his brother. Landon is serious, whereas everything is a game to Reed." Avery rested her head back and looked up at the blanket of stars covering the Texas sky. "I should have sent him home the minute he had arrived. He's not cut out for this."

Emily leaned against a post and lifted her mug to her lips. "Something tells me you couldn't have stopped him if you had tried."

"I could have tied him up." Avery chuckled. "I could have told his sister. There were a hundred ways I could have made him stay."

Emily walked over to her and patted her back. "You know, he wasn't interested when I came on to him. You should have seen his face." She chuckled. "He's got it bad, and I think you do too."

Avery shook her head at the thought. She liked Reed. She liked him a lot, but she'd never had it bad, and she wasn't about to start. "I'm just his babysitter, and a lot of good I'm doing. He almost died on my watch."

She turned to look at Emily and found Reed standing at the back door. A playful smile tugged at his lips. "Reed."

Emily glanced over her shoulder. "I'll just give you two some privacy."

"You know, I've always had a thing for my babysitters." He held Avery's gaze and licked his lips. "Another fantasy you'll have to fulfill right after the naughty maid and librarian." He winked before turning to Emily. "Does your sister use social media?"

"Yeah."

"Do you mind pulling it up? My computer is on the table."

"Sure." Emily walked back into the house, leaving Reed and Avery on the patio. The air between them was charged, and her heart clenched as she held her breath.

"You don't honestly think she'll post her location on social media, do you?" Avery grinned and glanced back up at the stars.

"She won't need to." Reed stepped out onto the porch and closed the door behind him. "All I need is to see her face and my ability kicks in."

Reed moved up behind her and wrapped his good arm around her waist before placing a tender kiss on her neck. "I can find her sister."

"What makes you so sure?" Avery asked, tilting her head to give him better access.

"I'm going to let you in on a little secret that no one else knows."

"I already know you're missing a few screws since you're interested in me," she teased.

"My computer ability extends beyond the actual computer." He kissed the dip where her shoulder and neck met on the other side. "When I meet people, regardless of whether I'm around a computer, little boxes appear that only I can see."

"That explains a lot. You're delusional."

He chuckled. "I can see their entire electronic fingerprint. Anything and everything they've stored online is at my mercy for inspection."

Avery's body stiffened. That wasn't possible. Maybe he was really a little crazy in the head.

"Explain."

"The boxes that pop up give me access to everything. Bank records, pictures, anything and everything they access electronically, I can get my hands on."

"There's only one flaw in your story." She turned in his arms to watch his eyes to determine if he would tell her the truth. "When you found me at the hotel. I didn't make those reservations electronically. I didn't use a credit card or my personal bank account. How did you do that?"

Reed stared back at her, a slip of a smile on his lips. "I hacked the hotels and searched their registries for new reservations."

"Then how did you know I'd be in Texas to even start looking there?"

"When Landon called, it was through an electronic device. I traced himthe way any FBI agent would. I hacked systems and triangulated his location. I had an idea where to start looking."

Avery's mouth parted. "The boxes? How do I know you're telling me the truth?"

He leaned in to whisper. His breath came out hot on her ear. "Your Nonnie's secret ingredient in her spaghetti sauce is cinnamon."

"How..."

"She only keeps recipes and family photos online." He pressed a kiss to her ear before stepping back and shrugging. "They pop up whether I want them to or not. It's a gift and a curse, and the only way I was able to break that code on the thumb drive that Landon sent."

Avery crossed her arms over her chest and tilted her head. "And how, exactly, do you think you're going to find Alice Page?"

"By looking at her face." Reed grinned and turned to leave, only to be stopped by Avery catching his good arm.

"What do you think you'll find?"

Reed shrugged. "I'll track her cell to start and then move to her accounts. I'll hack the hospital, her computer, hell, I'll even hack her security system, if she has one. I'm not going to leave any stone unturned. I am going to help find that woman if it means bringing Landon home."

Some might think Reed's words were

crazy or arrogant, but she wouldn't use those words to describe him. Determination was a much better word. As Reed walked back into the house, she realized right then one thing with absolute certainty. Reed wasn't the kind of guy to give up, on anything. Including the game for winning her heart.

"I'm so screwed."

****

Progress was slow as Reed made his way through the information in the boxes that popped up by staring into Alice's face through her social media account. Even Reed himself was creeped out by his ability. He shouldn't have been surprised by Avery's avoidance since he'd shared his secret. His shoulder ached as he repositioned himself so he could use both hands to type instead of picking at the letters with one hand. A quick glance at the living room clock told him what his body already knew. He would be in a world of hurt tomorrow if he continued to work. The house was eerily quiet. Every occupant was sound asleep. Reed was the only one still awake.

Reed pinched the bridge of his nose and clenched his eyes closed. The glow of his laptop screen started to mess with his head. He pushed the complaints to the back of his mind and concentrated again on Alice Page.

The woman was incredibly smart, working her way through med school by herself, never relying on anyone else. She was the brightest student and top of her class. As Reed continued searching her school records, he froze. Staring at him on the screen were two words he knew well. Computer Engineer. "I'll be damned."

Alice Page had a minor in computer engineering. His lips twitched, and his fingers moved faster over the keyboard with nothing more than a hunch. Ten minutes later, he ran his hands through his hair, ready to pull it out. He was so sure he'd find something to indicate she was the one responsible for the thumb drive heating system and codes. "It doesn't make sense."

"What doesn't?" a female voice answered back.

Reed glanced over his shoulder to find Emily standing on the threshold in nothing more than a nightshirt that hit her knees. She was a beautiful woman in her own right as she stood in the glow of the hall light, but Reed had eyes for only Avery.

"Does your sister like computers?"

"Yeah." Emily smiled as she approached and joined Reed on the couch. "She's a computer nerd. Growing up, she loved to tinker and create new things. We all thought that she'd go into that field one day."

"Why didn't she?" Reed asked and clicked back to Alice's social media page, looking at her picture in a new light.

Emily slid her legs beneath her bottom and rested sideways against the couch cushion. "She was in a car accident at the age of fifteen."

Reed's brows dipped, as he tried to piece the puzzle together. He came up short.

"It should have killed her. We still don't understand how she walked away. She had internal injuries, and that's when she found out she'd never be able to conceive. Never have a baby of her own." Emily took a deep breath. "She changed after that. She became more determined than anyone I know." Emily smiled. "She decided if she couldn't have one of her own, then she'd help other woman bring them into this world." Emily held Reed's gaze. "I think it was her way of dealing with a part of herself she'd lost. She's a fighter. That's what gives me hope that she's still alive."

"I'm so sorry." Reed's heart clenched at the thought of that right being stripped away from any woman. He couldn't imagine the damage that could do to a woman's psyche. "Is that why she quit toying with computers?"

"Oh, she still toyed. The last time we spoke she was talking about a new invention that involved a thumb drive. Her whole voice vibrated with excitement as she spoke. I hadn't heard her that happy since before the accident."

"A thumb drive?" Avery asked, walking into the room, wiping the sleep from her eyes.

"Something about how she'd created a thumb drive, similar to the nervous system." Emily bit her lip as if trying to remember. "Yeah, if they didn't have the right algorithm, there was a virus that would attack the mainframe, causing it to overheat."

"Son of a bitch." Reed stood and immediately regretted the hours he'd spent sitting on the couch. He paced the room to work the kinks out of his body. "Did she say how to stop the overheating without the password?"

Emily tilted her head. "She was talking over my head when she was explaining, but yeah, I think she said it was another one of her creations."

"What creation?" Reed asked, sitting back down. "Think, Emily, it's important. What did she create to combat the overheating?"

"A compression sleeve, like a patient would wear. It goes over the thumb drive.

She said it acted like acupuncture, pushing all the right spots to block the signal that the code sends to the computer to start the overheating process."

Emily stood and walked into the open adjoining kitchen to start a pot of coffee. "She said she was on the verge of getting a patent for both items, but I don't think she ever did before she disappeared."

"Something like that could be worth millions."

"I don't know about you, but I've lost a dozen of those little things in my life. What good is the information on it if you can't find it?"

"There's a tracking chip inside accessible by the user's platform," Emily called out as she stuck her mug where the coffee pot should be. "That was my suggestion."

"It still doesn't explain where she went or why. With all the used bloody towels we found lying around her house, I have to assume that it wasn't because of her computer toys, but more because she was a doctor, even if she only delivered babies. Stuart wouldn't have been interested in babies or electronics. He's only interested in two things, money and making more of it.

Reed met Avery's gaze, and they both spoke at the same time. "The ledger."

"What ledger?" Emily asked pulling out

her mug and replacing the coffee pot underneath the nozzle.

Avery was about to hurry from the room, but Reed stopped her. "We need to find that sleeve and take a short trip."

"What ledger?" Emily asked again, and they ignored her.

"We have it here." Avery's words were directed at Reed. "We crack the ledger, and we'll know what the hell she got into."

Reed cringed. "I was only able to decrypt half the drive. There was a portion I couldn't get to." He gave her an apologetic look; his secret would cost them precious time. "Another screen that required access was taking too long. It was heating up my computer, and the boxes weren't fast enough."

"You didn't tell me. I asked you exactly what happened, and you left that part out." Her voice rose in anger, and her eyes narrowed to slits.

"What boxes? What ledger?" Emily asked. "Will someone tell me what's going on?"

Reed turned to Emily. "I think your sister hid information on one of her thumb drives, and I believe if we figure out that information, we'll find her."

Emily's mouth parted.

Reed grabbed Avery's hand. "I'm sorry I didn't tell you. I was using it as my bargaining chip. But we need to find the sleeve and go back to the Island so I can crack the rest."

"No." She slipped her hand free. "We need to meet Landon tomorrow."

Reed dropped his gaze to his feet. Landon was the reason he was here, but he couldn't leave Alice running, not when he was so close to figuring out the secret keeping her away.

He lifted his head. "How about this? We go to her house tonight to look for the sleeve, and then we still make the plane to meet Landon."

"Or...how about this...I'll go look for the sleeve; you get some sleep, and we'll still meet at the plane."

"Avery, I've slept for two days straight. I couldn't sleep if I wanted to." He took her hand again. "I know what I'm looking for." He lifted his shoulder and then regretted it. "You can stand as my lookout, and we'll make it quick."

When she hesitated, he continued. "This could save her life, Avery. We have to do it. It's the right thing to do, just like what you did for Landon in the jungle."

"Fine." She pointed to the table. "Emily, we're going to need you to write down the directions to your sister's place, and then make sure our stuff makes it to the jet."

Emily grabbed a pen and pad. "Do you really think this is going to help find her?"

Avery walked to the stairs and stopped, her hand on the rail. "We won't know until we find the sleeve."

9 CHAPTER

Avery popped her clip and checked the bullets before shoving the weapon back into the waistband of her jeans. "Stick by my side this time," she said in a stern voice. "We aren't having a repeat of the club."

She glanced up at the two-story farm house and barn sitting on the property.

"It could be worse. She could have nosy neighbors."

"You've got a lot to learn, Love." She shook her head. "We're sitting ducks out in the open like this." She pointed to the clump of trees near the house. "Snipers could be set up there." She pointed to the barn. "The window at the top." She then lifted both hands to the house. "Hell, they could be waiting inside and we have no element of surprise. So let's make this fast."

"Emily said Alice's office is upstairs."

Avery sat back and took in their options. The barn door was slightly ajar. The surrounding fields were empty. Not an animal in sight.

Both the barn and the house were dark, the sun not due to rise for another hour.

"We'd cover more ground if we split up." Reed's voice was smooth, if not a little hesitant.

"No chance." Avery shoved the door open and stepped outside. "We stick together."

"Right," Reed mumbled and slipped out of the passenger door.

Thunder rumbled, and the wind caressed some of the heat from her face. Avery glanced up at the cloud-filled sky. The stars from earlier were nowhere in sight. A storm was brewing.

Avery slipped her gun out of her waistband and held it with both hands pointed at the ground as they walked toward the house, stepping up on the rickety porch. She slipped to the window and peeked around the frame. The house was dark, the furniture still broken on the ground.

Reed gestured to the splintered frame

around the lock. Whoever had come was determined. Avery squatted, getting a better look at the red splatters on the wood. Blood. Everything Emily had said was true.

Rising, Avery moved in front of Reed and lifted her gun. Using her toe, she opened the door and cringed from the sound. If the lights from the car hadn't announced their presence, the damn squeaky door did.

Without saying a word, she reached back, grabbing Reed's hand and moving it to her hip in a silent demand for him to stick close. Her finger rested on the trigger as she stepped inside. She'd been in situations like this countless times, but never with a civilian whose life rested in her hands. She took deep, steady breaths. The only sounds that filled her ears were the rush of her blood and the groan of the wood beneath her feet. The stench of burnt coffee lingered in the air.

She scanned the broken furniture as her mind tried to process what might have happened. The blood, the broken door hinge, and this. Whoever had come in, came in fast, catching any occupants off guard.

She eased up to the corner that led down the hallway, keeping her back to the wall; she peered down the darkened corridor. Empty. The broken furniture was contained in the living room. She stepped around the corner and tiptoed down the hall, systematically checking the rooms quickly and efficiently, just as she'd been taught.

"Now upstairs, then we'll start our search." Avery gestured to the ceiling and stepped out of the door at the end of the hall, quickly and fluidly moving to the stairs. With each step, she pointed her gun toward where someone might hide to take a shot.

Within minutes, she'd cleared the top floor, and they'd found Alice's office. She flicked on the desk light; a soft glow illuminated the oak surface.

Reed sat down in the chair and rummaged through the drawers while Avery picked up a file on the desk. She flipped it open. Empty.

She dropped it and picked up another. "Empty. Who keeps empty files on their desk?"

Reed stopped his search and picked up the file, reading the label on the tab. He tapped his finger on the label. The file had a number instead of a name. "Does that look familiar?"

Avery's brows dipped. "No."

"The ledger. I'd bet money that's one of the numbers on that ledger."

Avery shuffled some papers on the desk around, looking for something, anything that might have been in that file. "Do you think she knew they were coming?"

Reed shrugged his broad shoulder and went back to rummaging for the sleeve, and Avery moved to the bookcase and ran her fingers across the spines. Medical books and journals mingled with electronic books covering the real estate. Avery picked up a picture on a table in front of the window. Emily and another woman smiled brightly at the camera with the rolling waves and sand as a backdrop. They both sported tans. A family vacation?

Avery handed the picture to Reed and continued her search. If she were hiding something of value, she'd have a safe, or at least a hiding spot. She wouldn't leave it out in the open. Even without neighbors, Avery wouldn't have taken that chance.

"It could be anywhere." Avery scanned the surroundings, looking for anything that looked like a sleeve.

"When I was a teen, I used to hide things under my mattress," Reed said as he shut the drawers.

"That's a lame hiding space. All mothers know to look for porn there."

"All right, smarty pants." Reed rose from the chair. "What about you? Where did you hide your diary?"

"I didn't have a diary." Avery rolled her

eyes and walked to the door.

"Okay, how about tucked away in a shoe box or maybe a vent or loose floorboard?"

"Possibly." Avery turned to Reed. "You check her room, and I'll check the kitchen."

"What happened to no splitting up?"

"If you get in trouble, just scream and I'll come save you." Avery's lips twisted into a grin she didn't bother trying hide as she stepped out of the room and jogged down the stairs.

Avery had just stepped into the kitchen when an arm snaked around her waist and a large hand covered her mouth. Her shoulders tensed in response.

"Don't scream," Landon whispered.

The tension in her shoulders deflated.

They both heard the floorboard squeak, and before they could even turn around, Landon's hand disappeared. His body landed on the floor with a thump.

"Oh no." The candle holder slipped from Reed's fingers. "Landon?"

"Why did you do that?" Avery dropped to her knees and tapped lightly on Landon's face. "Come on, Lan, wake up."

"I thought you were being attacked. I came to rescue you."

Avery moved around Landon's body and grabbed his shoulders. "Help me get him to the couch."

Reed helped her carry Landon and dropped him unceremoniously on the couch. "Tell me this isn't the rendezvous spot."

Avery slid onto the floor to sit beside Landon. "Nope."

"Then what is he doing here?"

She was asking herself the exact same thing. One minute she'd been all teeth and grins, and the next, she was ready to bite the hand covering her mouth. "Probably the same thing we are, looking for clues."

Landon moaned, and his eyes slid open. He blinked several times and reached for his head. His eyes trained on Avery. "What did you do to me?"

"It wasn't me, slugger." Avery rose and held out her hand to pull Landon up. "You can thank your brother for that nap."

Landon's eyes widened as he stood. A pin drop could be heard in the room while the staring match commenced. "Avery?"

Avery knew that tone, the one that implied he was trying not to lose his cool.

"What is Reed doing here?"

"What do you think I'm doing here?" Reed's voice rose with each syllable. "Did you expect me to stay on the Island knowing you were in trouble?"

Landon ignored his comment and turned to Avery. "You brought Reed into danger? What were you thinking?"

Avery held up her hands and stepped

back. "I left him behind. I can't help that he followed me."

Landon released a pent-up sigh and rubbed the spot on his head. "We don't have time for this. Reed, you need to go home and let us take care of this."

"Right, because you're doing such a bang-up job." Reed stomped to the curtain and pulled it back. The sun was still below the horizon, but by the time they finished arguing, it would be daylight.

"You two can stay here and argue. I'm going to search the barn." Avery moved to the door and swung it open.

"No need. I've already searched the barn and the cellar." Landon's brows dipped. "That's where I was when you pulled in." He lifted a brow at Avery. "You should check the entire house before you assume it's clear. There's no sign of who took Alice."

"Maybe not, but that's not what we're looking for." Reed made to cross his arms over his chest and cringed at the pull on his stitches.

"You're hurt?" Landon's tone changed from annoyance to concern. "What happened?"

"He was shot," Avery answered.

"What the hell, Avery?"

"It doesn't matter," Reed reassured him. "In your search, did you find anything that was shaped in a letter L that could be used as a sleeve for the thumb drive you sent me?"

"Not that I remember." Landon shook his head. "Who shot you?"

When an answer didn't come, Landon turned his gaze to Avery. "Who shot Reed?"

"Come on, we'll explain everything on the way back to the safe house."

Reed rested his hand on Avery's back and walked her to the car. He could feel Landon's eyes on his back where he was touching Avery. Still, Reed didn't care.

Avery slipped behind the wheel, and Landon met him on the passenger side. Neither one of them made a move to get in the car, but she knew they were discussing her. Landon was probably trying to warn Reed, and if she knew Reed, he wasn't backing down. True Love boys down to their core.

She lowered the window in time to hear Landon tell Reed that whatever was going on was a bad idea. As if she didn't know already. There was no room for Reed in her working life, and that was all she had. Work, with the occasional trip home.

"Quit wasting time and get in the car," she hollered to both of them and waited until they were both in to roll the window back up. "For the sake of saving time, I've already warned Reed that I don't do relationships." She held Landon's gaze in the rearview mirror and could feel the worry from that single look.

Reed turned in the seat. "And I've already told her that I hear her loud and clear, but that I won't be derailed."

The mood in the car was thick with tension between the brothers. Landon, her best friend, and Reed, the man who'd been sleeping in her bed. There was nothing she could say to ease either of their minds. Inevitably, Reed wasn't going to be a part of her life, and so was the fact that Landon would never forgive her for crossing that line.

Landon leaned forward and rested his arms on the back of the seat as they informed him of everything that happened and what the thumb drive held. He was as surprised as she'd been to find out about the boxes that appear to Reed and the intricate security design behind the thumb drive.

A moment of hurt crossed Landon's eyes as Reed discussed his ability and the stuff he'd been picking up on everyone along the way, but to his credit, he remained silent until they were finished, never letting on what she could so easily read in his eyes.

"I should have come home more." Landon ruffled his brother's hair. "You could have told me what was going on with you."

"You should have come home anyway," Reed said as a response and turned in his seat to meet his brother's eyes. "We all worry about you."

Landon sat back in his seat. "As you can see, I'm fine."

"Far from it," Reed mumbled and turned back around. Landon remained quiet the rest of the trip back to the house as Reed and she tried to figure out where the sleeve might be. They had both been so sure it would be in that house. Stress built in her shoulders as they pulled up to the safe house. Light illuminated the shadows in the living room. Emily was seated in the rocking chair on the porch, sipping from a mug.

10 CHAPTER

Landon found Reed sitting on the dock. Reed had given them space and time to go over everything that had happened to Landon while he'd been on the mission and since.

"Avery tells me that you think one of the numbers on the file matches the ledger."

"Yep." Reed tossed a rock and watched the ripple on the water. Each ring extended farther when he switched the angle, kind of like finding Alice. With each step they took, they chipped away, looking for clues, making their presence felt a little further each time.

Landon slid down to sit next to him. "I'm sorry I dragged you into this. If I'd known you would have followed her, I never would have sent you the thumb drive."

"I'm not sorry." Reed tossed another rock and it sank beneath the surface of the water. "I'm a selfish bastard, just like you." Reed lay back on the dock and rested on his good hand.

"Selfish?" Landon asked. "Is that what you call someone trying to save a life?"

Reed finally looked at his brother. He was a trained killer and worked for a company that none of the family knew about, doing God knows what. Oh, that was right. He wouldn't know what the hell his brother was into. Landon never bothered to check in with him. Anger skirted his spine as Reed rose from his spot to stand over his brother.

"Did you ever for a minute think about what your absence is doing to our family? You weren't there when our sister walked down the aisle in our mother's dress, or when Olivia and Declan found out they were having a baby. You missed Flynn finally meeting his match, and what about Mom on her birthday? You didn't see the hurt in her eyes that you didn't even bother to fucking call. You can't ever get those things back. Those things make you selfish."

"What, because I have a life?" Landon jumped up from his spot. "I'm the job, Reed. That's who I am. And calling me selfish is like calling the kettle black, big brother."

Reed shook his head and had turned to stomp back up to the house when Landon grabbed his arm. "What are you doing with Avery? Hmm?"

Reed yanked his arm free. "That's none of

your damn business."

"You're putting her and yourself in danger just by being here. Her head isn't in the game. That was obvious when I snuck up on her at the house. You're going to get her killed, and why? Because you want to sleep with her? Are you hoping that one night in bed with you will convince her to settle for a life on the island? That you'll be able to give her a happily ever after?" Landon shook his head. "Take a good look in the mirror, Reed. You'll never give her what she needs."

The anger riding up Reed's spine turned to full outrage. He balled his hand into a fist and swung, knocking Landon right in the mouth and sending him off balance. His arms flailed as he flew off the dock and landed with a splash.

Reed spun to find Avery standing on the end of the dock with her arms crossed.

"Avery..."

She turned her cheek and held up her hand as Reed passed. Was she as aggravated as him? Good. Reed stomped up into the house and into his room. He knew when he wasn't wanted, and he damn well wasn't going to be sticking around with that little prick. He had a life to go back to, even if he wasn't dragging Landon's ass home with him.

***

Landon climbed up on the dock. His shoes squished and his clothes dripped, and Avery's palms itched to shove Landon back in.

Unsure why—maybe it was the daggers she was sending him—Landon lifted his hands. "Now just wait."

Avery pressed her lips together, ready to kick Landon's ass.

"I had to know that what I was picking up on about his feelings were true. I only said that to see his reaction. I had to know for sure."

"You had to know what?" she asked through gritted teeth.

He took a tentative step in her direction and stopped out of arm's reach. "Av, I don't know how to tell you this, but Reed is falling for you, and not just in a crush kind of way. He's falling hard."

Avery dropped her arms to her sides. "This was a test?" She stepped closer. "Your brother risked his life to find your sorry butt, and this is how you repay him?"

"We've been best friends a long time, Av. I don't want either of you hurt, so if this is just a fling, you've got to end it now. Save the guy some dignity and cut him loose."

Avery threw her hands up in the air when she really wanted to choke some sense into her best friend. "You have no idea what you're talking about. It hasn't even been a week since we started our hunt to find you." She shook her head. Landon was playing some twisted game.

"He punched me because of you."

"No, I'm pretty sure it was all because of you," she countered. "He's angry, and from the sound of it, he has every right to be."

"Oh, so now you're going to side with him?" Landon asked incredibly. "I have a job to do, Avery. I work. That's who I am. I'm not pretending to be someone I'm not."

"You think I'm pretending!" Avery clenched her fingers into a fist.

"We live for the job." His voice softened, as if he was placating her. "That's who you are, too, so don't go fooling yourself that you'd be happy on the Island for a long stint."

"The only one pretending here is you, Landon. You're pretending that your actions aren't hurting your family. You're pretending to give a shit about something that you, yourself, couldn't care less than two rats' asses about." She stepped into his face. "You're a lot of things, Landon, but I never thought you were a dick....until now."

Avery swiveled around and stormed off, slamming the back door on her way into the house. How dare he even suggest she was the one pretending?

****

Reed glanced up to find Emily standing in the doorway. "You're leaving?"

Reed shoved another shirt into his bag

and disappeared into the bathroom on a hunt for his toothbrush. "Yep, I can report back that my brother is still an asshole."

He rounded the corner to find Emily had stepped into the room. "You can't go yet. We haven't found Alice."

Her eyes searched his, and he tried his best to ignore the plea in her eyes. "Landon says I'm getting in the way."

"Since when do you care what he thinks?" She plopped down on the bed and laced her fingers in her lap. "Alice is a lot like your brother and you."

She glanced down at her laced fingers. "Her job is her life, like Landon, but she cares, like you. She spent more time at her clinic than she ever did at home or the hospital." Emily gave a sad chuckle. "That's why she doesn't have any animals on her farm. She was afraid that she'd forget to feed them."

"Her clinic?" Reed slipped his toothbrush into his bag and paused. "I thought she had an office next to the hospital."

"Alice divides her time between all three places, but her heart has always been at the clinic. She tries to help everyone: teens, battered woman, anyone that needs help." Emily looked up at him. "She's a good person, Reed. The most kind-hearted person you'll ever meet, so please don't go. Please help us. Please. If you won't do it for Landon, then do it for all the women she helps, please."

Reed ran a hand over his face. The thought of working with Landon left a sour taste in his mouth. Not that he didn't love his brother, but right now, he was ready to throttle him. "Tell me more about her clinic."

11 CHAPTER

Reed jogged down the stairs with Emily on his heels. Avery was sipping coffee at the kitchen table while Landon was leaning against the counter, holding a bag of frozen peas to his lips. Hitting his brother had been wrong on so many levels, and still, it had felt good deep down. His baby brother needed a lesson in family values. Reed pushed the thought aside.

"We need to go," he barked out. "Where are your keys?"

He glanced around the kitchen and swiveled on his heels to look in the living room.

"Where?" Avery rose.

"The clinic," he muttered while still

searching the table for the keys.

"What are you talking about?" Landon asked.

"Reed thinks we might get information at the clinic where my sister spends all of her free time."

"What clinic?" Landon's brows dipped before he turned and tossed the bag across the kitchen to land with a thump in the sink. "She doesn't own a clinic."

"Yes, she does," Emily answered. "Well, technically it's owned and named under a non-profit organization that has several free clinics throughout the country, including some overseas, but she runs the local one."

"Why didn't you tell us?" Avery asked, slipping the keys out of her pocket.

"I already went there and spoke with Janice. She's the manager and my sister's right hand. She hadn't heard from her either."

"Less talking, more walking," Reed announced, moving to Avery and grabbing her hand, pulling her toward the door.

"We'd be going in blind. It's dangerous without a plan. Have you checked out the place online?" Landon asked, moving to block their exit. "I'm sure you can access their files without going to the building."

Reed tilted his head and lifted his brow. *Seriously?*

"The website is still up for the international clinic, but the local files were taken offline." Reed reached around his brother and opened the door. "In other words, if I want to get into their files, we need to go there, and we're wasting time. Either you're in or out, Landon. Make up your mind."

"You aren't going anywhere without me."

"Or us," Rick and Sam announced as they jogged down the stairs and turned into the living room. "But Landon is right."

"Finally, someone who agrees." Landon grinned.

"We aren't going anywhere without being prepared," Sam said, turning to Avery. "Grab your gear, your comm, and your gun." He gestured to the stairs. "Since they know Emily, she can get access to her sister's office and look for the sleeve. Avery and Reed, you guys can go in as a couple and find a computer access point."

"Fine by me." Reed grinned and grabbed his backpack and laptop from the table, in the event he needed them. Avery jogged up the stairs and returned a minute later.

"My brother isn't going in. He doesn't even know how to shoot."

"But he knows computers," Avery answered, coming down the stairs. "He'll do the work, and I'll relay on the comm." She stuck the plastic piece in her ear. "If we run into any problems, we'll call you in."

Reed opened the door and slipped into the same SUV that they'd driven to Alice's house.

They needed answers, and he was hoping the clinic could provide them just that. Reed logged into his computer and used his phone's hotspot to access the Internet. He sent a quick text to his brother-in-law, Luke.

Found Landon. Not sure if I can get him home, but tell the others he's okay. I'll have your jet back tomorrow.

He'd just shut the screen when Avery, Landon, and Emily joined him in the car. Landon was behind the wheel with Emily riding shotgun.

****

Landon glanced up at the tiny brick building that looked like a throwback from eras past. The red brick was crumbling, and the banner above the door was faded. "Do they even have Internet?"

Emily turned in her seat. "Yeah, don't let the appearance fool you." She grinned. "The inside had a complete overhaul to get it up to code before they could open."

Reed slid his computer into his backpack and got out of the SUV, meeting Avery around the front. He slipped his fingers through hers. "Are you ready?"

"Of course." She smiled until they walked inside the clinic.

They stood just inside the doorway as men and women walked around, carrying things in boxes.

"Uh." A woman wearing a nametag with Janice scrolled on it greeted them. Her hair was frayed and falling from her clip. Her face pale white, and the boxes popping up around her face were telling. A picture popped out like a target on a dart board. Stuart Franklin and she were in a bed taking a selfie. "We're closed."

Reed glanced at the reception desk. No computer in sight. "Closed for good or are you just moving?"

Janice clasped her hands together. "Closed for good," she said apologetically. "There's another clinic about five miles from here if you need medical help."

A big, beefy man crossed the hallway with a computer in his hands, and Reed desperately wanted to follow.

"Thanks for your help," Avery offered and turned to leave. As they stepped out, Avery pressed the comm in her ear. "Send in Em, and make it fast. They're tearing the place apart. Sam, get me eyes on the vehicles loading the files and equipment."

Emily smiled as she passed, heading into the office like a woman on a mission. They should have come sooner. The thought churned and settled into Reed's stomach like rust on the coils of a car battery. Whatever clues they could have found would soon be gone.

Reed opened Avery's door and waited for her to slip inside before taking his seat next to her.

"Well, that was unexpected," she mumbled to herself.

"You can say that again," Reed mumbled.

Landon turned in his seat. "Do you think they're trying to hide something?"

"She's having an affair with Stuart Franklin."

"What?" Avery's mouth parted as she stared at him. "Emily didn't tell us that."

"She probably doesn't know, but I'd say they intimately knew each other." His mind raced, trying to put the pieces together. "Stuart Franklin is in this up to his neck. The question is whether Janice was a willing accomplice."

"She can't be convicted of having an affair. What else did you see?" Landon asked.

"That was all I had time to dig into."

Reed propped his elbow on the window and rubbed at his jaw as he stared at nothing particular, trying to make sense out of what had happened.

"Let's hope Emily has better luck than we did."

"Alice is missing, yes, that's horrible, but why would they just shut down? Why not bring in another doctor, unless somehow Janice or the agency is involved?" He glanced at Avery.

"This is a missing person, not a homicide. There isn't a crime...yet."

Reed turned his head back to the window. "Yet."

Ten minutes later, Emily emerged from the building, carrying a box. Picture frames and a small plant stuck out above the rim. She wiggled her brows up and down in quick succession with a grin on her face. The drive back to the house seemed as though it took forever. Reed struggled not to climb into the back and look through the stuff.

****

Emily emptied the contents of the box on the kitchen table. And Reed was fast to grab the neoprene sleeve in the shape of an L. He studied it, running his fingers over the groove on the inside. "This is it."

Reed plopped down in a chair, studying the design.

"I'll go with Reed back to the Island while you two keep an eye on Janice," Avery announced and glanced at the others. "I want you two to break into wherever they're storing the computers and patient records, and take the contents somewhere safe until we get back."

12 CHAPTER

Reed settled into the plush leather seat on the jet as they reached their cruising altitude. He examined the sleeve, wondering exactly how Alice had manufactured the object. The construction and intricacies of the little spokes that would stop his computer from overheating were ingenious. Why did she need it? Alice was a doctor. A computer encryption would have saved her patients' files from prying eyes, but this....this was something else. He could feel it in his core and knew whatever they uncovered wouldn't be good.

"What's rolling around in that thick head of yours?"

"Pandora's box," he answered. "Are we sure we really want to know what Alice went to all of this trouble to hide?"

"If it helps find her, then yes," Avery said reassuringly, sliding the sleeve from his fingers she placed it on the table next to her drink. "Reed...I know you weren't expecting

119

any of this, but I wanted to thank you for your help. I don't think we could have gotten as far as we have if it hadn't been for you."

"I'm not sure Landon would agree."

"Landon means well." She shrugged and lifted her cocktail to take a sip. "He's worried you'll get hurt...again."

"And you're not?" His lips twitched as he slid his fingers through hers.

"Of course I am." She squeezed his hand. "I care about you, Reed, but you have to know that this"—she lifted his hand—"this won't go anywhere."

"Yet you haven't pulled free."

She leaned across the seat, and her hot breath mingled with his. "I'm enjoying it while I can."

He cupped her head and pressed his lips to hers, stealing her breath and her words. This wasn't a fling, not to him, not by a long shot. He held her while he savored her, tasted her. She tasted like a delicious cinnamon roll, telling him the contents of her drink were Fireball and cream soda as she melted into his touch. Every fiber in his body was strung tight with need. The plane jolted, breaking their connection as they heard Henry's voice come over the speaker.

"Mr. Love, there appears to be a storm hovering over the Island. We're being grounded on the mainland until it blows through."

Reed raised the shade covering the window as Avery moved back into her seat, pulling the seatbelt tight. Rain pelted against the glass, and the jet dipped, causing Reed's stomach to flip. Not good. He glanced at his watch. Four thirty. They wouldn't make it in time to get into the safety deposit box.

"Looks like you'll be enjoying our time a bit longer than expected." He glanced at her, hopeful that his next words didn't cause her to freak. "The drive is in my safety deposit box, and we won't be able to get it until Monday."

"Please remain seated and buckled in as we make our approach," Henry called over the speaker again. "We're flying in the outer bands of the storm, and this may be a bit bumpy."

Bumpy was an understatement, Reed thought as he held his stomach while standing in the cabin waiting to disembark. The muscles in his fingers were stiff from holding the armrest so tightly, which pulled the stitches in his shoulder. His stomach churned as he stood on shaking legs. Avery was still laughing and wiping the tears from her eyes as the engine died and Henry stepped out of the cockpit toward them.

"I've talked to the tower. They expect the storm to move past through the night. So we're going to be stranded until daybreak."

"Thanks," Avery offered when she found

her composure. "Are there any hotels close by?"

"There's one about ten minutes away. I've arranged a car service to take you there."

****

Three hours later, after having checked into the hotel, ordering room service, and bathing together, Avery was lying against Reed's stomach, enjoying every delicious ache in her body from their latest tryst in the tub as he flipped through the television channels.

"What do you think we're going to find on the drive?" she asked, glancing up at Reed's face, taking the time to admire his strong chin and the dimple in his cheek.

"Medicare fraud?" He shrugged. "Or maybe it's hush money. She won't tell that some rich guy has a contagious disease."

Avery grinned and rested her head against his chest. "How about an account in the Caymans she set up in order to run away with her lover? Ohh, no, I know. It's payment for a hit, and all those files lead to people who were killed in the operating room."

Reed stroked his finger through her hair. "Whatever it is, we know it can't be good. Look at the lengths she went through to make sure no one could read it."

"True." She kissed his chest. "You know, when we get back to the Island tomorrow, we're going to have to stick together for the next few days." She smiled to herself. "That means you have to see Nonnie again."

Reed kissed her forehead. "Then you get to come to my mom's for Sunday lunch."

Avery's mouth parted. Meeting his family wasn't part of the deal. The fewer people who knew they were together *together,* the better. Nonnie wouldn't judge her for bringing a man home, but his... "I'm not so sure that's a good idea."

"You aren't scared, are you?" Reed chuckled.

Avery rose to her knees and straddled his hips. "I'm not scared, but what are we going to tell them? Hi, I'm Avery. I'm sleeping with your son and putting him in danger while my best friend...your other son... is leading a secret double life."

Reed sat up, resting his palms on her waist. "We tell them the truth. I'm helping you with a computer issue, and as far as a relationship goes, it's not any of their damn business. We're still in the getting-to-know-each-other phase."

"We're way past the getting-to-know-each-other phase," she whispered against his lips before kissing him until his head was back against the pillow.

Reed smiled up at her, and his eyes sparkled. "I'm not sure I know you thoroughly enough."

Avery leaned over and trailed a path of kisses down his neck.

"What's your favorite flower?" he whispered.

"Lily," she answered and worked a path down his chest.

Reed cleared his throat. "Favorite meal?"

"Nonnie's spaghetti."

She moved lower with each answer.

"Favorite movie?"

She glanced up and grinned. "*Titanic.*"

"Why?" he asked. "Because she gets the necklace?"

"Nope." She kissed lower and moved to slide his track pants off his legs. "It's my favorite because, in the end, when she's lost everything, she still lives like there's no tomorrow."

Avery grabbed the hem of her shirt and lifted it off her body, tossing it on the floor before she settled over him again. Lifting his cock, she slid down on it, making Reed groan. "Oh yeah."

She rose again and slid down, letting him fill her until she was fully seated. She leaned over. "Enough with the questions."

He nodded and lifted his hips. "Enough for now."

****

They made love several times throughout

the night, and Avery fell asleep in the early morning hours. Her hair tickled his chin and chest. Her breath warmed his skin. The scene would have been beautiful if it weren't for the sound of her snores competing with the thunder rumbling outside the window. Even that was cute in a way only Avery could make it.

Reed stroked her hair and smiled as her next snore came and went. His heart ached like the stitches in his shoulder. How was he supposed to forget how she made him feel? How she made him want things he'd never known he'd missed? Her boxes were easy to ignore. He didn't want to delve into her secrets. He enjoyed talking to her and finding out the hard way.

He kissed her head again. He had two days to convince her that he was worth taking a chance on. That he wasn't like any of the others. Two days to win the heart of a woman he wasn't ready to let go. All of this was new to him, foreign like the engine of a car. He was going to need help, and he knew exactly where to get it.

Reed closed his eyes and let the sounds of her snores and the thunder outside lull him to sleep.

13 CHAPTER

The private airport on the Island was nice and deserted, leaving them with a quiet lull. The torrential rain that had passed through had left everything fresh and alive. The smell of the surf and trees nearby reminded him why he loved this place and had never left.

Reed shoved his key in the ignition, and for a brief moment, enjoyed the lack of apprehension that had been riding him the last few days. "You know your snores sound like thunder."

Avery's mouth parted at the audacity of his accusation. "I don't snore."

Reed leaned over, in his car on the Island, and kissed her. "It's okay. I sleep better when there's a storm."

"You're trying to butter me up." Avery's

smile lit up her face.

"Well, you are meeting my family this weekend, and there's no telling what horrid stories they'll come up with to share."

He tossed the gear into drive and drove out the gate. "So what are the plans?" he asked, glancing her way. "You staying at my place this weekend, or are you going to tease Nonnie that you're in a relationship and we stay there?"

"Definitely your townhouse, but I do want to see Nonnie. So how about we spend a day with her?"

Reed went to his house, showered and changed clothes before they drove to Avery's house. Nonnie was at the door when they pulled up. Her face lit up like a kid on Christmas morning.

"I see you found her and persuaded her to come home."

Reed paused at the door and kissed the woman's cheek. "Yes, ma'am."

"Good." Nonnie gave a terse nod and headed back toward the kitchen.

"I'm going to shower and change," Avery announced following Nonnie to the kitchen.

"I'm going to step out back and make a couple phone calls to the family and check in," Reed said stopping at the counter.

Nonnie patted his cheek. "You're a good boy."

"Don't let him fool you, Nonnie." Avery

chuckled and turned to head upstairs.

"You know better than that, child. I may be old, but I don't fool easily. He is a good boy. I can see it in his eyes."

She watched Reed as if reading him like an open book. "Go, make your calls." She nodded again and turned to work on the dough she had laid out on the counter.

Reed stepped out the patio doors and continued down to the beach, where he kicked off his shoes and sat down on the sand, watching the waves crash against the shore.

He dialed his brother-in-law first. Luke picked up on the third ring.

"I hear you made it back."

"I did. Actually, we did. I'm with Avery."

There was a pause on the line. "Did Landon come with you?"

Reed had known the question was coming, and try as he might to come up with a plausible excuse for the family on why Landon stayed away, he failed miserably. "No, he's in the middle of something. Is Sky around? I need to talk to her."

"Sure." Luke's voice was muffled as he hollered for his wife.

"Hello?" Skylar answered.

"Hey, squirt."

"Reed." Her tone rose an octave. "How did it go? Did you talk him into coming home?"

"I'm sorry, Sky. I tried, but you know how stubborn Landon can be."

"Oh." Reed heard the disappointment in her sigh.

"But that's not why I'm calling. I need help."

"Help?" she asked, her voice perking up. "I'm good at help."

Reed grinned. "There's this girl..."

"Ahh. You need *that* kind of help. I can do that. Where are you?"

"I'm at Avery Malone's beach house."

"Avery, huh? I wouldn't have paired you two, but stranger things have happened."

"Well, she apparently doesn't do relationships, so any pairing on your part would have been a waste of time."

"Every girl longs for a strong, loving relationship, so anyone telling you differently is blowing smoke up your butt."

Reed rose and dusted the sand off his shorts. "Tell me more."

"Show interest in the things she likes. Connect with her on a level that makes her feel special. Just be yourself."

"Show interest, make her feel special. Got it. Any other advice?"

"Get to know the real her, what makes her tick, what makes her smile, and do more of that. Reed, relationships are hard, but it's the people that make them worth working at. Is she worth the effort?"

"Yeah." He smiled, and his heart clenched. "She is."

"Perfect," Skylar answered excitedly. "Bring her to lunch tomorrow."

"I will." Reed turned to head back toward the house. "Oh, and Sky, thanks."

"That's what family is for. We'll see you tomorrow."

Before he hung up, he stopped her. "Could you do me one more favor?"

"You're pushing your limit," she teased.

"I need some lilies tomorrow. I'd like to surprise her."

"Anything else? Maybe an engagement ring?"

Reed chuckled. "I'm not trying to send her running. Just the flowers for now."

"You've got it."

"Thanks, Sky. Love you."

"Love you too," she answered before the line went dead.

Reed glanced up to find Avery on the porch. "Love you? Is there something you're not telling me, lover boy? You got a girlfriend I don't know about?"

Reed stepped up beside her. "Is that a hint of jealousy I hear?" His lips twitched as he pulled her into his arms. "You're the only girl for me, Avery. It would be easier if you'd just accept that."

He lowered his lips to hers in a soft and sensual kiss. "Why don't you go surf? I'm sure you could use a break from me."

"Really?" she asked and glanced longingly

at her board. "But..."

"I'm not going anywhere. I'm going to hang out with Nonnie. Go." He grinned. "Have fun. Maybe when my arm is better, you can teach me how, and we can do it together...when you're in town, of course."

"Of course," she echoed before disappearing into the house.

Reed made his way into the kitchen to find Nonnie kneading dough. "Whatcha making?"

"An apple pie for dessert tonight."

"Would like some company?"

Nonnie looked at him as if it was a trick question.

"Avery's going to surf for a while."

"She's leaving you to go surf? I thought I taught her better than that."

"It was my idea. She's put up with me the last few days. She's due for a break, and besides, if I'm going to win her over, I should know how to do more than boil water, right?"

Nonnie grinned. "You can cut the apples."

They worked in easy banter as an hour passed, first one and then two. The pie was in the oven, and she'd moved on to teaching him everything he needed to know about how to make homemade meatballs, including sharing the recipe to her special sauce.

She'd asked about the bandage peeking from beneath his shirt, and he'd deflected the question by asking one of his own. She'd poked and prodded for information about his life and what he did for a living. How many brothers and sisters he had and his family life. This woman wasn't shy about anything. She reminded Reed of an older version of Avery. She was saucy, extremely keen and perceptive. There would be no fooling this woman.

"Do you love her?" she asked while putting the meatballs in the oven.

Reed paused, grabbing the spices from the cabinet. "I like Avery, but I haven't known her long enough to love her," he answered as honestly as he could.

"When I met Frank, God rest his soul, I was the same way. Do you know what made me realize that I loved him back?"

Reed leaned against the counter, all thoughts of what spices she needed were gone. "What?"

"He was willing to walk away in order for me to be happy. It wasn't until he did that I knew I couldn't live without him."

"You're a wise woman," he answered and grabbed the spices. "Although Avery strikes me as the kind of woman who would just let me leave."

Nonnie chuckled and patted his good arm as she took the spices out of his hands. "Her heart is as big as the sun, my boy. She gets her smarts from me." Nonnie winked and added some spices to the crushed tomatoes in the pot.

14 CHAPTER

Avery toweled off the salt water from her face and glanced up at the house. The sun was high in the sky, and her time in the water had been worth whatever embarrassing stories her Nonnie might have told. She'd needed the peace. She needed to get her head back in the game, and the water was where she found her solitude, most days.

What had she done by letting Reed into her life? She liked Reed. Even if he was a delicious temporary distraction, he was still a distraction. The way he watched her, his gentle touches, and his hot kisses, would she ever be ready to give all that up?

"Crap," she mumbled to herself and grabbed her board. She sat the board on the patio and hosed off the sand sticking to her legs and feet. She stepped into the house and paused.

Reed was in the kitchen with Nonnie. They were both laughing and cooking together, a sight that made Avery's heart clench. She never brought anyone this close to Nonnie, afraid of what her grandmother might say when they disappeared out of her life.

"What's so funny?" she said as she approached.

"Nonnie was just telling me about the first time her mother tried to teach her to cook."

Avery's heart expanded. She knew that story, all too well. Nonnie had burnt the lasagna, including the bread. "Is that what's for dinner?" Avery asked, lifting the lid on the pot. "Did you let Reed cook?"

"We cooked it together," Nonnie answered, grabbing water out of the fridge and handing it to Avery. "You two can take the leftovers when you go back to his house. It makes an excellent midnight snack."

Avery met Reed's gaze. He'd told Nonnie they wouldn't be staying. She didn't know whether to be mad or impressed. Most men wouldn't have been as honest and would have hemmed and hawed about their situation.

"We're going to be working," Avery explained. "Please don't make more of us spending time together than what it is."

"Working, right, dear." Nonnie pulled the pie out of the oven and turned to Reed. "Could you give us a minute?"

"Sure," Reed answered and gestured with his thumb toward the living room. "I'll just go and make another call."

Nonnie waited for Reed to leave the kitchen and step outside. She planted her hands on the kitchen counter. "I see the way he looks at you. I'd be blind not to."

"Nonnie, it's not like that."

"Avery." Her tone gentled as she stepped around the kitchen island and rested her hands on Avery's arms. "Honey, he's a good man, so I'm going to give you a little piece of advice that my mother gave me."

This should be interesting. Avery's brow rose.

"You can travel the world and do everything your heart desires, but wouldn't it be that much better doing those things with someone you love at your side?"

"Nonnie, Reed's life is on the Island," she said, trying hard to hold the woman's knowing gaze. "We're too different."

"Like the sweet taste of cinnamon and the acid taste of tomatoes." Nonnie grinned. "They are on opposite sides of the spectrum but still find a way to work when put together."

Avery's mouth parted, the comeback stifled in her throat.

"Just keep an open mind, Avery. Men like him are worth experimenting with to see if the flavors mix."

"Nonnie," Avery gasped.

****

Avery carried the plastic container of leftovers into Reed's house. Their late lunch had been delicious, and she had no doubts the leftovers would be just as good. "You made an impression."

Reed shut the door and locked it behind them. "I had fun. Nonnie is a wise woman. And don't worry, I didn't tell her to start planning the wedding."

"You two looked chummy." Avery walked into the kitchen and opened the fridge, moving stuff around so the containers would fit.

"Someone needs to keep an eye on her while you're off saving the world." Reed slid up behind her and put his arms around her waist. He placed a kiss on her neck. "You do it for me every time you see Landon. It's the least I can do in return."

Avery turned in his arms and laced her fingers behind his neck. "You're not supposed to be this perfect."

"I'm far from it, Avery." He smiled. "I have an ulterior motive." He leaned in to kiss her. "I'm saving up brownie points." He winked. "For when you get the full Love experience tomorrow with my family."

They spent the rest of the evening together, watching television and talking. Only once did Reed log onto his computer to send out a few emails about projects he'd been working on. The rest of the time he devoted to her and making her feel at home.

The night went by with no threats looming over their heads, no guns pointed in their direction. Just the two of them relaxed and carefree. It saddened her to think of what she'd been missing as she pondered Nonnie's earlier advice. Would this make her happy? Only she could answer that, and she wasn't ready to concede. Not even for Reed.

15 CHAPTER

Reed placed his hand on Avery's back and guided her across the lawn to the front door. He leaned into her ear. "Are you nervous?"

"Nope. I've dealt with hitmen and mob bosses as part of my job. The Loves will be a piece of cake."

Reed grinned at her misguided confidence but kept his comments to himself as he pushed the door open and guided her toward the voices in the backyard.

His sisters-in-law, Olivia and Mia, were sitting with Skylar and his mom at one of the umbrella tables. Their easy banter ceased the moment they spotted Reed and Avery closing in.

"You must be Avery," his mother said by way of greeting as she rose and pulled Avery into a hug.

Avery's brows dipped, her body stiff under his mother's assault.

"Come join us." She guided Avery away from Reed and glanced over her shoulder at him. "You can help the boys while we get to know your friend."

"Play nice, ladies." Reed gestured with his fingers from his eyes to theirs as if he would be watching. Reed grinned at Avery's wide eyes which pleaded for him to stay. He winked and left her to fend for herself.

****

Avery sat on the edge of her seat while all the women at the table stared at her.

"You know Reed's sister, Sky."

Sky nodded and smiled.

"This is Olivia, Declan's wife, and that is Mia, Flynn's wife."

"It's nice to meet you all." Avery smiled, ignoring her fight-or-flight feeling. She'd met strangers before, including killers and assassins, but Reed hadn't been joking. These women were in a whole different ball game.

"So." Sky leaned forward and clasped her hands together. "Reed and you?"

Avery's mouth parted.

Oliva nudged Skylar.

"Give the woman a second to breath," Mia said with a smile. "You guys can be a little intimidating."

Avery cleared her throat and glanced across the yard to find Reed watching her. "Reed and I are just friends."

"Just?" Olivia prodded as she rubbed her belly. "There is no *just* anything with the Love boys. You either love them, or you're ready to kill them. There is no in between."

"Now that's not true." Mia picked up a glass and took a sip. "You were friends with Flynn."

"No," Olivia corrected. "I was friends with Skylar, and Flynn was just looking for a way to aggravate Declan."

Mia sipped her drink and continued watching Avery, studying her as if she was a specimen. Her gaze started at Avery's short hair and traveled down her face before she glanced down at Avery's flip-flops. "You're local. A beach lover, if I had to guess by the tan."

"You don't guess," Olivia teased.

"You're right, I don't." Mia set her glass down and leaned forward. "Short hair means you're probably low maintenance. The indentation on your finger suggests that you not only own a gun but you also practice with it regularly. You have a bruise on the inside of your arm and your physique and toned muscles support my theory that you're not only active but a fighter. Which, truth be told, I already knew when you came to the apartment to pick up your bag of guns." She grinned. "Your quietness, while we unceremoniously grill you, tells me that you're used to keeping secrets."

Avery pressed her lips together and narrowed her eyes at Reed.

"And that look"—Mia leaned back with a grin and pointed toward Avery—"tells me that he's getting under your skin."

"Mia dear, not everyone wants to be analyzed." Reed's mother reached over and patted Avery's hand. "You'll have to forgive Mia. She's works in research, and she has a hard time turning it off. Avery, you don't need to tell us anything you don't want to."

Avery took a minute to process these women. There was certainly more to them than met the eye. All of them were smart and calculating, which meant she would have to switch tactics from the nice-girl routine she'd planned in her mind.

"Mia's right, about all of it." She grinned. "I carry a gun for my job; I surf every chance I get, and I'm used to keeping secrets." Avery nodded in Mia's direction. "And Reed..." Avery looked across the yard to find him helping his father near the grill. "What woman in her right mind wouldn't realize that he's a good guy?"

"Every woman but you," Olivia said.

Avery met her gaze. "Even me. But that's not what we're about. Not that it's any of your business. You guys can sit here and judge me on your observations, and I somewhat understand that. I'm a stranger here with someone you love. I'd probably do the same thing in your shoes. But I can also say I'd probably do it with a bit more class and be less obvious. Whatever this is that's happening between Reed and me is none of your damn business, not that there's anything to tell." Avery stood and glanced between the women. "Are you guys always this rude to the women he brings home?"

Mia's smile grew as though she held the answers to the universe, and she wasn't ready to share. "I like her."

"Me too," Olivia mumbled. "Reed doesn't bring home women."

"We had to know," Skylar announced, easing up out of the chair with her hand on her baby bump. "I'm sure you understand. He's my baby brother. Please forgive us for being bitchy."

"It's a hormone thing," Mia said.

"What's your excuse?" Olivia chuckled.

"My excuse? I'm just blunt." Mia rose.

"What exactly did you have to know?" Avery asked Skylar.

"That you'd fit in." Skylar patted Avery's arm. "Welcome to the family."

"What just happened?" Avery mumbled.

"They like you," Reed's mom said, winding her arm around Avery's.

"I'm not sure I like them," Avery said, making Reed's mom chuckle.

"They'll grow on you." Reed's mother steered her toward the back door. "You get an extra helping of pie."

Not sure why the woman thought an extra piece of pie would make a difference, but one bite and she was in heaven. Any torture the other women had given her was worth the taste of heaven in her mouth. She closed her eyes and savored every single bite.

16 CHAPTER

"Your family is missing a few screws," Avery called over her shoulder, moving things around in the fridge again to make room for the additional leftovers.

"Tell me something I don't know," Reed answered, walking down the hall to change out of his clothes. His smile grew as he glanced around his bedroom. Dozens of bouquets of lilies were placed around the room and covered the dresser, and petals covered his bed. Skylar had gone all out. Reed grabbed a single lily and carried it out into the living room.

Avery was lying on the couch with her arm resting over her eyes.

"Tell me they were nice to you."

She moved her hand and raised her brow. "If that was nice, I'd hate to see when they're mean."

"That bad?" he asked, lifting her feet. He sat on the couch, placed her legs over his lap, and handed her the flower.

She smiled, lifted it to her nose, and inhaled. "No wonder you needed brownie points. You didn't tell me they were angelic piranhas." She chuckled. "Your being single makes sense now. I'm not sure any other woman would have passed the test."

"Angelic piranhas?" he asked.

"Sweet and innocent like angels with sharp teeth, ready to tear you into two with smiles still on their faces."

"Are you sure we're talking about the same women? Skylar, Olivia, and Mia wouldn't act like that. That is so out of character for them, even with them being hormonal."

"Ha," Avery said. "They would and did." Her eyes softened. "But pie made it all better." She held up her flower. "And this."

"If you like that, you'll love what's waiting for you in the bedroom." He winked and rose, holding out his hand to pull her off the couch.

She opened the bedroom door and stepped inside. Her face lit with a smile, and her eyes sparkled as she moved throughout the room, leaning in to sniff the flowers. "If I didn't know any better, I'd say you were trying to sweep me off my feet."

Reed chuckled. "That might be a little difficult with one good arm, but I'd be willing to try."

Avery took his hand and pushed him to sit on the bed. "The bank opens tomorrow."

Reed's heart squeezed tight. "I know."

She straddled his lap, her knees on the bed. "Make love to me."

"Don't you mean sex?"

She shook her head. "It's probably our last night, and I want the memory to carry me through all of my tomorrows. Make love to me, Reed."

Reed crushed his lips to hers without a second thought and spent hours branding memories into her mind. If he couldn't have her in a relationship, there was no way in hell she'd forget him. Ever.

****

Avery used her sunglasses to cover the bags under her eyes from the lack of sleep. Her muscles ached and her legs felt like noodles. She let out a deep breath when Reed laid his warm palm on her lower back. The comforting heat from his touch warmed her to the core, melting some of the ice still left around her heart.

Reed guided her to the customer service desk and slid his license across the shiny surface. "I'd like access to my safety deposit box, please."

"Certainly, Mr. Love." The woman behind the counter gave him a genuine smile as she typed in the computer with the phone pressed against her ear.

Within minutes, the branch manager walked out. "Right this way." He gestured with an outstretched hand, guiding him to the room where Reed's bounty was held.

Reed waited until they were alone before he pulled out his box with the duplicate copies of what he'd printed and the flash drive. He stuffed the contents into his backpack and slid the box back into the slot, locking it.

"Do you think this is going to work?" she asked as they made their way out of the bank and to his car.

"I hope so." The ride back to his house filled her with apprehension, the air thick and foreboding. She braced herself for whatever they might find.

Reed locked the door behind him before grabbing the sleeve and wrapping it around the thumb drive. He went to work, pulling numbers out of thin air to populate the security boxes waiting for him and bypassed the information they already had. When a screen popped up with a skull and crossbones, he went a bit slower throughout.

"It's not heating up," he mumbled more to himself then to her.

"That's a good thing, right?"

He smiled up at her and she leaned down to kiss him, as if he needed it for luck. The screen instantly populated with several file boxes. Each one was a duplicate of the number on the ledger.

"Here goes nothing." He clicked on the first box and paused. Pictures of a baby swaddled in a pink blanket in a hospital nursery. A predominant birthmark in the shape of a heart on her tiny cheek. The name attached to the crib said Miller. He scrolled past that screen to another picture. One of a woman in a hospital bed, holding the baby with, presumably, the father smiling down at the two. The next one had the baby's birth certificate with the delivering physician's name at the bottom. He pointed to it. "Alice didn't deliver this baby."

He flipped to the next screen of a different woman holding the same baby. Sunglasses hid the woman's face as she glanced over her shoulder with a baby in her arms.

The next picture was a close-up of the baby in her arms. The birthmark was unmistakable.

"Oh, crap," Avery whispered, her hand covering her face. "Either that baby was stolen, or sold."

Reed flipped to the next screen. A snapshot of a bank account with the baby's birthdate and amount highlighted. The name on the account was Janice Monroe. Reed glanced away from the screen before pointing to the depositing account number. "This one belongs to someone named Wilson Hutchison."

Every fiber of her being turned to ice. "He's a mob boss in New York."

He pointed to it and flipped the screen again. This time, it was a missing poster of the same baby with the birthmark.

"How?" he asked and lost his train of thought. "If Alice didn't deliver these babies, how is Janice involved, and how did Alice get her hands on this?"

Avery had her phone out and walked across the room. "Sir, we have a situation." She spoke in hushed tones before she hung up and dialed again. "Landon," she said with urgency in her tone, "I don't have time to explain, but you need to detain Janice, and search her house and every property she owns. She's either behind Alice's disappearance or knows who is. Pick her up now."

Avery watched in horror as Reed clicked open the rest of the files. Each time he got to where money was transferred to Janice, he'd mumble another name, each individual worse than the one before. Powerful men in office, underground drug lords, and even a senator had made that list.

"Alice must have figured out what was happening." Avery pulled up a chair and plopped down before she fell. "Probably had the intention to go to the FBI."

Reed clicked open the last file and her heart dropped. Another baby swaddled in a blanket. Alice was written on the side of the crib. A single note was on the next page. "I know who you really are, do you?"

Reed leaned back in his chair, his mouth agape. "What do you know about Emily's family?"

"They were rich socialites and died in a car accident when Emily was sixteen and Alice was eighteen."

Her eyes searched the screen for clues.

"Do you even think either of them was blood-related to their parents? This suggests that Alice might be a victim like one of these stolen or sold babies."

"I don't know." And that was the truth. If this information was a bombshell to her, imagine what it would do to Emily and Alice.

"Print that for me. Copy it and keep it safe. I have a rendezvous with a team that is going to show up in thirty minutes, and we don't know who we're dealing with."

Avery paced the living room, biting her nails as Reed went to work doing everything she asked. She moved to the window several times and peered outside.

"Whoever sent that to her"—Avery shivered, taking the documents from Reed's hands—"and those poor babies and parents..."

Avery's stomach dropped. The consequences of this information would destroy lives. She couldn't even imagine the implications when these kids found out they didn't belong to the people that had stolen them.

"One thing is for sure. If Alice is still alive, she's going to be the target of a lot of angry, powerful people who have unlimited resources. She's going to need a hell of a lot of protection."

Reed cupped her cheek and pressed his lips to hers. "You'll protect her. That's what you do." The smile on his face didn't reach his eyes. "Avery, I love you, and all I ever want is for you to be happy."

"Reed..."

He gave a slight shake of his head. "Go conquer the world, kick ass, and save lives. I'll still be here waiting, if you come back. I'll wait for you forever."

"Forever is a long time," she whispered into his lips.

"Yes, it is." He let out a shaky breath and kissed her once more.

"Reed, promise me you'll forget about me. Don't spend your time waiting for me to come back. I won't."

Reed answered her with nothing short of the hottest kiss she'd ever receive. His mouth, his hands, his taste... He touched and tasted every part of her down to the core of her soul. This was his goodbye. On some level, he must have known she'd said the truth, that things between them wouldn't last, yet he kissed her like a man fighting for the right to breathe.

Avery broke the kiss and stepped back. Tears welled in her eyes as she clutched the documents in her hands. Her breath was labored with each step. "Goodbye, Reed."

He gave her a slight nod and Avery walked out the door without looking back.

17 CHAPTER

First one week went by, then two. Reed went back to life as usual, combating computer viruses with less zest than he normally exuded. He missed Avery. He missed her smile, her sarcasm, and her kiss. A call from Landon was the only way he knew they'd found Alice chained up in Janice's basement, barely alive. His company and the authorities were tracking down the children in the file and the families they had been stolen from. The emotional task turned out to be hard for everyone involved. The news reports filled up with powerful people being hauled off to jail, the mob boss sneering at the camera as if he'd get revenge. The death threats had started. How Alice's name had leaked, no one had a clue. The only thing good that came out of the situation was Landon was coming home. Only this time, he'd be returning with a doctor in tow. Alice had her very own personal bodyguard. Reed attempted a smile. Landon deserved that headache and much, much more.

Landon's advice on the phone that day was short and to the point. "Forget Avery and move on."

As if that would ever be a simple feat.

Reed ducked out of family meals, not ready to answer questions about a relationship that had been doomed before it began. He immersed himself in work, surfing the net to track down thugs like the child molester, when he'd first got the call from Landon.

Stuart Franklin and Janice had each been arrested and the media had suggested that the FBI was digging into the parent company to see what else they might find.

Reed held a small hope that all of the wrongs would be righted and Avery would come home. Who was he kidding? He shook his head. She wasn't ever coming back.

A knock sounded on the door. It was probably just another brother or Sky sent to pull him out of his slump. He swung the door open, the words already flying from his lips. "I said I'm fine."

The man standing on his stoop was dressed in a suit, his hair slicked back. "Good to know."

"Can I help you?" Reed asked, his tone turning agitated.

"No, but I can help you." He nodded as if asking permission to go inside.

Reed remained firm, blocking his entrance, and crossed his arms over his chest. "Who are you?"

The man laced his fingers behind his back. "I'm Mr. Pate."

As if the name alone was supposed to ring a bell. Reed tilted his head.

"I'm Landon and Avery's boss."

Well, now that was an answer he hadn't been expecting.

"Neither one of them are here," Reed said, dropping his arms to his sides.

"I'm well aware of that, Mr. Love. I'm not here to see them; I'm here to see you." He gestured to the house again. "Are you going to invite me in, or shall we have this conversation on the stoop, for all of your neighbors to hear?"

Reed opened the door and stepped back, letting Mr. Pate cross the threshold into his sanctuary.

Mr. Pate stopped in the middle of the living room and turned, scanning his surroundings, his face unreadable as he glanced at the computer.

"Please have a seat." Reed gestured to the couch.

"This won't take long." He slid his hands into the pockets of his dress pants. "Reed, I have a proposition for you."

This was sounding more cryptic by the second, but the man held Reed's attention. "I'm listening."

"After four years in my employment, Avery has been reassigned to the Island."

That was news to Reed. His whole body vibrated at the thought. "Okay. That doesn't sound like something she would have wanted."

"Trust me when I tell you that it was not only what she wanted but exactly what she needs." Mr. Pate lifted his chin. "That's where you come in."

"I don't understand." Reed propped his hands on his hips. "What does Avery coming home have to do with me?"

"As you know, Landon is accompanying Ms. Alice Page to the Island for her protection, and Avery is his handler. It makes sense that she be close by for an extraction, if necessary."

"Okay, still not sure what this has to do with me."

Mr. Pate paced the small space. "I'd like to hire you to work with Avery."

Reed's mouth parted before he snapped it shut again. "Work with her how?"

Mr. Pate gestured to the computer. "Ms. Page will be working at the Island Hospital under an assumed last name as part of her protection. She's managed to rattle the cages of some very powerful men. In her duties at the hospital, Ms. Page will be in contact with several patients, and in turn, Landon will be providing around-the-clock security. He will be her shadow."

"You're still not answering my question."

"I understand that you all have unique abilities." He paused. "The extent of which is even being kept from me, but I understand the need for privacy. Ms. Page will be fully equipped with a tracker and a video recording device. There have been numerous threats to her life, and should you decide to accept my offer, your job would consist of doing a background dossier on everyone who she comes in contact with."

"If you're that worried, why are you letting her work in the hospital?"

"I see you haven't met Ms. Page, or you wouldn't be asking me that question."

"What makes you think I can do what you ask?"

"Avery believes in you. That is enough for me."

"Does she know you're here? That you're suggesting this?"

"Of course. She made a point of picking you and said something about, if I didn't, she'd turn into an angelic piranha."

Reed's lips turned up at the corners.

"I'd like to talk to her and think about it before I make my decision."

"Of course." Mr. Pate took a card out of his pocket and handed it to Reed. He went to the door and made a gesture. "I look forward to working with you."

He stepped out of the house, and Avery appeared in the doorway.

"You asked for this?"

Avery walked in and closed the door. "I figured it would be easier this way."

"What would?"

She walked over to him and slid her arms around his neck. "I thought it would be easier if my husband and I worked together."

"Husband?"

She smiled up at him. "You are going to make an honest woman out of me, aren't you? I'm not sure Nonnie would be very happy if you didn't."

"Anyone ever tell you that you're pushy?" he asked, placing his hands on her hips and leaning in to kiss her.

"I've taken tips from the angelic piranhas." She smiled. "I wasn't out of town a day and realized I'd left something behind."

"What, Avery? What did you leave behind?" he asked, hopeful and hesitant.

"My heart. I love you, Reed."

Reed rested his head against hers. "Remember who said it first." He kissed her with the pent up passion he'd been storing for her return. Taking a breath, he pulled back. "Now I can tell Nonnie to plan the wedding."

"I already have," she whispered.

Reed chuckled. "And what if I didn't take you back?"

"It was inevitable, and I would have chipped away at your resolve." She pressed her body up against his, letting him know exactly how she'd planned to do it.

"I love you," he whispered against her lips.

"I love you back," she answered.

The End.

Thank you for taking the time to read my stories. As always I appreciate each and every one of you. If you liked it and have a moment, please leave a review on Amazon.

Keep reading for a sneak peek of Landon's book, now available on Amazon.

LANDON

Chapter 1

This assignment would be gravy they'd said. Keep the target secured by any means necessary. Not a problem. Those commands were words Landon Love lived by. He'd actually been smug about getting some downtime from the flying bullets and operatives who tried to get the upper hand. His superiors had left out one tiny vital fact when they'd sold him on the assignment. The place he'd have to take her to was the last place on earth he wanted to go. The one place he'd spent years avoiding. Home. Love Island to be exact. Local population, not counting tourists, three hundred and thirty-four, and every damn one of them knew his name.

Landon slowed his steps next to Dr. Alice Page. His gaze travelled up and down the white sterile corridor. Every muscle in his body was strung tight as he took in patients and visitors, assigning a potential threat level to each. His stomach was tied in knots. The uneasiness in his gut wasn't because of the job or even the barrage of emotions rolling off the hospital visitors and staff that made his breathing difficult. His nerves stemmed from something much worse—"having to face the family he'd been avoiding for the last seven years.

Landon tugged at the collar of his shirt, making room to swallow around the lump in his throat. *Stay focused.*

Alice regarded him with somber curiosity, as if silently trying to figure him out. He'd become used to seeing the same look in her eyes, day in and day out, for the last two weeks. Today was no different.

"Things could always be worse. We could be hiding in some no-name city and stuck in a safe house with no windows."

She playfully nudged his shoulder as if trying to lighten the mood. It wouldn't work. "We have the whole Island as our playground, and you have friends here. People you trust, not to mention your family. I'd call this a win even if you're saddled playing bodyguard for me."

Family. Landon's stomach churned, and the throbbing in his head intensified. His brother Reed had probably tattled to his siblings and parents that he was back by now.

Reed didn't know how to keep his mouth shut. It was inevitable and only a matter of time before one or all showed up.

"I'm not here for a family reunion, Doc." He was here to work. Still, it wouldn't be long before they cornered him into Sunday lunches. Truth was they deserved an apology or two, or a million. Every family had that one odd person who didn't fit in. Landon was theirs, and he'd lived up to the cliché in every sense of the word. He was the black sheep, the odd man out. Whatever you wanted to call it. Landon was the Love who filled that role, and he performed it with expertise.

"Only one more appointment and then we can leave."

"You don't have any more meetings on your schedule." He should know. Each person, each meeting, was vetted through the team assigned to keep her alive.

"It was a last-minute thing."

"All of your patients and meetings go through Reed so he can do background checks. You know the drill. There is no such thing as a last-minute anything where you're concerned."

"This one isn't a threat."

Alice reached for the door to her office, and Landon placed a restraining hand on her arm, effectively stopping her. "Thinking like that will get you killed. They're all threats until Reed, Avery, or I say otherwise. I'll go in first. You know the drill."

"I don't think that's necessary, but if you insist." Alice lifted her fingers to her forehead in a mock salute. It was better than the one finger goodbye he'd seen her give the last operative that she'd run off. Her lips twitched as she stepped back letting him open the door.

"Seriously?" Landon narrowed his eyes, angling his displeasure at the doctor who had just played him.

Alice stepped in behind him. "Mrs. Tanner, Mrs. Love."

His sister, Skylar, and their sister-in-law, Olivia, both rose with their hands on their backs, trying to get out of the plush fabric chairs that brought deep-chair sitting to a whole new level. Their pregnant bellies led the way.

"Dr. Parks, it's lovely to meet you." Skylar smiled and welcomed Alice with a handshake.

"Sky? What are you doing here?" Landon's brows furrowed as he closed the door behind him with a quiet click. His nightmare had officially begun. Not one Love but two.

"It's good to see you too, baby brother."

"We're just here to meet the new doctor," Olivia answered, giving him a sugar-sweet smile, trying to lessen the tension in the room. It didn't work.

Skylar held out an envelope to Alice.

"What's this?" Alice asked and slid her finger beneath the envelope flap.

"Your own personal invitation to Reed and Avery's wedding," Skylar explained. "I know Avery would like you there, and well...we all know Landon has to stick by your side. Where you go, he goes, even if he doesn't want to. I just wanted to make extra sure he didn't miss this one like he has all the rest."

Landon could feel the weight of his sister's stare challenging him to deny the truth of what she said. His suspicion was confirmed. His brother Reed, indeed, had a big mouth.

These two had an agenda, which was as evident as the twinkle in their eyes. And, God help him, the good doctor was like putty in their hands. Landon watched Alice's curiosity take hold. She was intrigued, which meant only one thing. Landon was fucked.

A wave of disappointment emanated from Alice and washed over him, clinging to his skin and soaking into every pore. His chest tightened at the familiar feeling, one he hadn't experienced in years.

Alice gave a little nod. "I wouldn't miss it for the world." She moved closer to Landon's side. "I don't know if you guys know this or not, but Landon, Avery, and Reed are the reason I'm still alive."

Skylar and Olivia exchanged a look that spoke volumes about what they *didn't* know.

"That's classified, Doc."

"They're your family, Landon. We can trust them." The disappointment flowing through the room and suffocating him swished away, lightening the pressure in his chest and easing his breath.

"Of course you can trust us, and you can tell us all about our baby brother's heroics during Sunday lunch at our parents' house." Skylar smiled in that *you-are-not-getting-out-of-this* kind of way.

"Oh I don't know…"

"Go ahead and give in, Alice. Skylar can be persistent." Olivia grinned and rubbed her belly. "Besides, if we're all going to be friends, you should at least get the chance to know us before you see us go into labor. I have a feeling we'll be sprouting horns when the pain kicks in."

A smile formed on Alice's lips, which quickly slipped when she met Landon's gaze. "Uh…sure. We'll try?" Her answer sounded like a question. Good.

"That's good enough for us." Oliva took Skylar's elbow, leading her toward the door. Just a few more steps and they'd be out of sight and hopefully out of mind.

Skylar grabbed the knob, turning at the last second. "If you can't make it, then maybe we'll come visit you." Skylar winked.

As quick as Landon's hopes rose, they were dashed just as fast. He knew better than to underestimate his big sister's determination. She was going to dig in her claws and try her best to keep Landon firmly grounded on this damn island.

The door clicked closed. "They seemed like nice people."

Looks could be deceiving. The truth was he honestly didn't know what to think of his family anymore. He'd been gone so long and he'd changed so much. Maybe they'd changed too. The occasional conversations between him and Skylar had grown shorter over time, not because of her but because of him. She'd always had a way of picking up right where they'd left off, as if the emotional strain between them vanished with each hello.

"I'm sure they are."

A twinge of guilt, hard and unyielding, lay buried in his chest. Not enough to get him to stay, but it sat there just the same. Alice was silently watching him again, like she normally did, trying to help everyone but herself, as if missing a few of the puzzle pieces to make it whole.

"I don't think us staying on the island is a good idea. They're a distraction."

"They're your family."

"That's my point. I should call in a transfer to a new location."

His jaw clenched, and his eyes narrowed as a mischievous grin appeared on her face. "Lighten up. It can't be that bad."

Text KATE to 313131 and get a text message on release dates!

Sign up for her newsletters at
www.kateallenton.com

Other Books by Kate Allenton

Suggested Reading Order
BENNETT SISTERS BOX SET (Books 1-4 in one bundle, 1218 pages)
INTUITION (Book 1)
TOUCH OF FATE (Book 2)
MIND PLAY (Book 3)
THE RECKONING (Book 4)
REDEMPTION (Book 5)
CHANCE ENCOUNTERS (Book 6)
DESTINED HEARTS (Book 7)

PHANTOM PROTECTORS BOX SET (Books 1-4 in one bundle, 964 pages)
RECKLESS ABANDON (Book 1)
BETRAYAL (Book 2)
UNTAMED (Book 3)
GUIDED LOYALTY (Book 4)

CARRINGTON-HILL INVESTIGATIONS
DECEPTION (Book 1)
DEADLY DESIRE (Book 2)

SHIFTER PARADISE BOX SET
NOT MY SHIFTER/ SINFULLY CURSED

KARMA

SOPHIE MASTERSON SERIES/ DIXON SECURITY
LIFTING THE VEIL (Book 1)
BEYOND THE VEIL (Book 2)
VEILED INTENTIONS (Book 3)
VEILED THREATS (Book 4)

THE LOVE FAMILY SERIES
SKYLAR (BOOK1)
DECLAN (BOOK 2)
FLYNN (BOOK 3)
REED (BOOK 4)
LANDON (BOOK 5)
ALEXIS (BOOK 6)
GABE (BOOK 7) COMING SOON
JACKSON (BOOK 8) COMING SOON

HELL BOUND

MYSTIC TIDES BOX SET

About the Author

Kate has lived in Florida for most of her entire life. She enjoys a quiet life with her husband, Michael and two kids.

Kate has pulled all-nighters finishing her favorite books and also writing them. She says she'll sleep when she's dead or when her muse stops singing off key.

She loves creating worlds full of suspense, secrets, hunky men, kick ass heroines, steamy sex and oh yeah the love of a lifetime. Not to mention an occasional ghost and other supernatural talents thrown into the mix.

Sign up for her newsletters on her website at www.KateAllenton.com

She loves to hear from her readers by email at KateAllenton@hotmail.com, on Twitter@KateAllenton, and on Facebook at facebook.com/kateallenton.1

Visit her website at www.kateallenton.com

Visit Coastal Escape Publishing's website at www.coastalescapepublishing.com